…there is beauty in the dark

NASTASIA BOTHA

Copyright © 2018 Nastasia Botha

ISBN 978-0-620-80937-5

First Edition

Cover designed by Destiny Productions

The Dark

Dark waters run deep…
I was never made for the shallow end,
When I dive, I dive in steep
Not ashamed to bleed
For as long as it runs crimson
And pulsates like a drum
I will not fear
Conquering the struggle of being alone
I rise a victor savouring the sequestration of peace

1

S asha made her way into the world, on the lounge floor of her grandmother's house, screaming and crying.

"It's a girl," the chubby old midwife dressed in plaid overalls declared before swaddling the baby in white towels and placed her on her mother's chest.

Her big brown focus running over the scene, settling on the eyes of her mother, who was drenched in sweat, from the immense energy she had spent birthing the 4.75 kg baby girl, who lied suckling her fingers, as they locked gazes. For in that brief moment, there was peace, there was warmth, and there was love.

By all accounts, Sasha was an easy child. Rarely cried, only when hungry and smiled most of the time, fascinated by all the colours, shapes, and people around her.

She grew in size right before your eyes, doubling her birth weight in just under a month. Her bald head covered with the slightest layer of fluffy black fur, her sparkling eyes always searching, with a drool-worthy smile, exposing her dimpled cheeks.

"What a beautiful big boy you have," people would comment to Sasha's mother's dismay, prompting the need for piercings at the tender age of 6 months old.

As is customary in the coloured community, Sasha earned the nickname: "Koppe", because her hair still refused to grow an inch. Lord only knows why the most absurd names were chosen, but since it was normal practice, it was widely accepted.

Her hair finally grew at the age of two. Shiny black locks framing her face like a fedora, as if it had always been there. She loved the feel of them bouncing on her head as she skipped, or the feel of her mother running her fingers through her hair. As it grew she liked it less, when her mother combed and plaited it. Sitting crossed legs on the floor, as mom pulled the comb through the knots.

"Sit stil," her mother would command, as she wiggled, trying to get away from what she perceived as pure torture.

"Ek weet nie wat sou jy gedoen het, as jy kroes hare gehad het nie," her mother would reprimand. She always wondered why she had to be grateful, straight hair or not, it was still an agonising process which left her feeling like peeing in her pants.

Always feeling different, she tried to navigate her life, searching for answers, finding enjoyment between the pages of books. She imagined herself as the characters in the stories she read. It made her feel free, since she always felt trapped by her awkwardness and insecurities; borne by the conservative nature of her upbringing. Her relationship with her mother dwindled; they seemed to have nothing in common and nothing to talk about. In fact Sasha always wondered if they were from different planets. She could not even comfort herself by hoping she was switched at birth, since she was born at home.

Her parents never spoke about love, relationships, feelings, or even sex. She tried making friends with the girls from school but it always inevitably ended in a competition that she had no knowledge of. Even amongst a room full of people she felt alone surrounded by darkness.

A darkness which stayed with her wherever she went, only allowing brief intervals when she lost herself in the stories she read.

2

High school...
"Hullelujah," she was exuberant being free from the tedium of childhood. Thinking that this would be where she found herself, found her place in the world. But even with a smile spread across her face, she struggled to relate, always feeling different. She tried different sports and finally found a home playing hockey, goalkeeping to be precise. She loved the rush of seeing the girls charge toward her, the adrenaline pounding in her ears, the risk of injury, readying herself for impact, placing herself between the charge and the goalpost at all cost, it made her feel alive.

As the natural progression, Sasha started noticing boys, tall boys, big boys, handsome boys, boys in all shapes and sizes. She would admire them under her lashes on the field during their fitness training, careful to not be spotted. All the girls had boyfriends by this time and she was left wondering what they had, that she clearly lacked.

"Why is my nose such a bolletjie, Ma?" Sasha asked her mother one Saturday afternoon as she washed the dishes, while her mother cooked. The smell of curry powder and jeera wafting around the kitchen.

Her mother stole a peek over her shoulder, laughter in her gaze, "Your father and I, ons het nie genoeg geld gehad om jou brug te bou nie." She laughed looking back to the chicken curry cooking on the stove.

Sasha rolled her eyes, biting her tongue and continued drying the crockery, before heading back to her room. Looking at herself in the mirror, turning from side to side, she felt deflated. Throwing herself on the bed, lying with her head on her arms. From nowhere she felt the urge to write something, anything. Like when she was a child after receiving a diary as a birthday present.

She sat with a notebook and pen in her hand, crossed legged on the bed, looking out through the window, the August wind bending the trees to its will. She listened to the tap-tap-trickle of sand being thrown against the window, as her mind floated and she felt again the same darkness she had always felt, envelope her.

Dear Diary, she wrote and laughed out loud. She felt like an idiot, but something compelled her to continue.

Why am I so weird? Why can't I fit in anywhere? My hare is te glad vir sommige mense en te kroes vir anders.

She exhaled slowly and stole another glance out the window. She imagined tumbleweed rolling across the lawn, thinking back to primary school when mean girls pulled her pigtails singing, "Ching-Chong-China," all the other kids laughing and pointing.

Girls are so mean and yet all of them have boyfriends while I am invisible, noticed by none. Can I blame them? There's nothing special about me, I can hardly notice myself. Who am I?

She closed the notebook, stuffed it into her schoolbag and took a seat on the edge of the bed looking through the window once more, lost in thought.

High school dragged by and left her feeling more and more invisible. Oh, she made friends, plastered a smile across her face, laughed at the correct moment. Supported a friend during a break-up, but deep down inside in her soul, she knew that nobody really knew who she was. Her parents assumed that she was happy; she played the part and nailed the lines.

To the world, she was a beautiful girl, with long black flowing hair, a smile that lit up the room with bright eyes, athletically built of average height; but standing by the mirror, all she saw was the sadness in her soul and questions in her eyes.

3

A nd then, it happened…

He happened! At the end of her matric year, after hockey practice, sitting on the floor removing the protective gear, "Duck!" someone screamed.

She looked up from the laces of her kickers, that she was untying, to see what the commotion was about when, BAM!

Time seemed to slow down to a crawl, she heard the ball slicing through the air, the gasps from the onlookers, she saw the light bend around the ball and still there was no way of avoiding the impact. The ball hit her head, right above her eyebrow, with enough force, it knocked her down. Lying on the cold grass as searing pain tore through her body, reverberating from her head down to her toes like a Mexican-wave. Tears poured from her eyes uninvited, as her dark sense of humour chose that moment to make its presence known, she burst out laughing. She thought of how strange it was that someone yelling duck always had the opposite effect. And, naturally she had to be the one in the firing line. She was always in the firing line, some cosmic joke; the universe was playing on her. Always clumsy, getting hurt, tripping over her own feet, walls suddenly appearing in her way. She cupped her eye with her right hand as she continued lying on the grass looking up through the blur her tears created. Her laughter quickly sobered by the faces looking at her, forming a circle around her, clearly questioning her sanity.

"Are you okay?"

"Sasha?"

She heard her team-mates ask, but their voices were indistinguishable. Trying to get up, she took the hand extended to her and before she knew it she was pulled up and stumbled into the arms of the boy who had lifted her. "Oops, sorry," Sasha quickly apologized but his hand was still clutching her elbow, steadying her. She peeked up at him, still clutching her face with her hand.

The world stopped spinning as she locked gazes with two brown eyes, like muddy pools, their depth evident, set in a handsome face, a face she recognized at once but a person she had never spoken to before.

"Roger!" Her mind screamed lips silent as she struggled to find her voice.

"Are you okay, Sasha?" Roger asked softly, searching her eyes.

Sasha giggled a little as embarrassment washed over her, turning her cheeks pink, ears overheating. "mmh," she said and looked down trying to break the spell his eyes were casting on her. "I'm fine," she answered and then quickly removed her hand from her face and immediately saw a trickle of blood smeared on her palm.

She wiped her hand off on her shorts as Roger lifted her chin, "you're bleeding." He observed.

"Yes, it's nothing," she said and added, "*thank you captain obvious*," in her thoughts, rolling her eyes and immediately regretting it when a sharp pain stabbed through her brain. The voices of the other people around her started breaking through. Fixing a smile on her face, she looked to each one to reassure them that she was fine; even though the throbbing in her head was intensifying.

Roger let go of her arm then and took a step back. She cringed internally imagining that she probably repulsed him. She could not begin to imagine what she looked like.

The other girls gathered her gear insisting that she sit down for a minute. She obliged and watched them scatter about, packing it into her oversized kit bag, while she shot glances at Roger, on the far side of the grandstand, trying to be inconspicuous but failed to evade locking gazes with him once more.

"Thanks guys," she said feebly, "I think it's best if I go, my dad will be here soon."

"I'm really sorry, Sasha. David asked if he could borrow my stick and before I knew it, the ball hit your head," Stacy apologised once more.

Sasha waved her off, getting up avoiding eye contact with Stacy, dusting off her bottom. "Don't worry about it Stacy, thanks guys." She lifted the oversized kitbag and walked to the parking lot and watched as her team mates dispersed while she waited for her dad. She was so happy the coach had already left before the accident because that would have meant a panicked call to her mother and an unnecessary trip to the emergency room.

She giggled, "no wonder they called me Koppe, my dik kop kan seker nie eers breek nie."

"What's so funny?" she jumped at the unexpected question and tug on the kitbag.

"Roger," she yelped embarrassed.

"Let me carry this," he pulled the bag off her shoulder, "you need a ride home?"

Sasha looked at him, "oh, no my dad will be here in a minute. Thank you," and released the bag to him.

He smiled a crooked smile looking down at her. She felt self conscious looking down as her gaze ran over his bare legs, in his soccer shorts and blushed.

"Are you sure you're okay? That was one hell of a hit."

"Yes, I'm fine," she looked up at him under her lashes before continuing, "it hurt, I have a throbbing headache but it's really not that bad." Sasha answered.

"Geez, you have a high tolerance for pain," he commented.

She turned her focus on him questioningly, "what do you mean?"

"You're strong, that's all," he stated and put the bag on the ground in the parking lot.

Sasha wiped her hand over her hair nervously, "thank you."

They were both silent for a while, "you don't have to wait with me, my dad will be here soon."

"I don't mind, besides I can't leave you here alone injured."

"How chivalrous of you."

Roger laughed carefree, "chivalrous, seriously?"

Sasha blushed, running the meaning of the word through her mind before she spoke again, she suddenly felt unsure, "what's wrong with that?"

"Nothing, it sounds good. It's refreshing having a conversation with actual words."

"Oh, how do you converse without actual words?"

He looked down, kicked a pebble and laughed silently before answering, "I mean using proper words and not slang."

"oh duh," Sasha said and unthinkingly smacked her forehead with the palm of her hand and immediately regretted it, as the pain that was throbbing in the background suddenly spiked. She closed her eyes tight with a sharp intake of breath.

"Are you okay?" Roger asked with his hand hovering.

"Yes, sorry. I forgot I got hurt. I'm fine," she answered feeling a little silly. "Thank you for waiting with me," she said as headlights of a car entering the parking lot swept over them, "my ride is here," gesturing to the approaching car.

"Any time," Roger said as he picked the kitbag up, the car came to a halt right in front of them. Sasha's father's gaze running over the boy standing next to his daughter.

"Hi Honey, have you been waiting long?" His eyes still trained on Roger, just a sideways glance too Sasha.

"No, Dad, not that long."

Roger extends his hand, "Good evening, Mr. Peters."

"Good evening, uh?" Her father shakes his hand, looking from Roger to Sasha.

"Oh, sorry. This is Roger, Roger this is my dad. Roger was waiting with me; I got hit in the head with a ball."

"What?" Her father's eyes shoot to her, washing over her, fixing his focus on the cut on her eyebrow.

Sasha lifted her hand, "I'm fine, it's a small cut."

"Let's get you home," her father insisted opening the passenger door for Sasha.

"Thank you, Roger," she said sliding into the seat.

"Yes, thank you Roger. Do you need a lift home? Can you put the bag in the boot?"

"No thank you Sir, my car is over there" and turned to put the bag in the boot as Mr. Peter made his way around the car to get into the driver's seat. Roger stopped short, "I'll see you tomorrow, Sasha."

"Oh, okay. See you tomorrow."

She sat back in the seat and watched Roger walk over to his car parked under the lamp, his calve muscles contracting as he walked, her gaze moved up over his body and settled on his back, his soccer shirt hugged the v-shape like a glove. She was still staring when he turned around and met her gaze. He smiled that same crooked smile that she liked, waved and unlocked his car. Sasha sat silently while her father drove away.

"Maybe I should take you to the doctor?" Her father said thoughtfully.

"I'm fine dad, it's not that bad. I just have a bit of a headache."

"Okay, then."

At home, Sasha quickly drank the two painkillers her mother gave her, after examining the wound. Quickly stripping down and getting into the shower. She stood under the faucet and let the hot water cascade over her face and body; the scorching water leaving her skin with monotonous blotches of red.

Wrapped in a towel after her shower, she sat staring at nothing in particular in her room, her mind racing, running over the entire encounter with Roger.

I didn't even know that he knew my name, weird! He is so sweet, she thought.

"Sasha, dinner's ready." Her mom called from the kitchen. Sasha donned her pyjamas, heading for the kitchen leaving her thoughts floating in her room.

4

S asha rushed getting ready for hockey practise the
following day. She had never been this excited for
anything in her life. Oh wait, she thought about her matric
farewell. How disappointed she was, when her partner
dropped her like a hot potato two weeks prior to the event.
It had taken all the guts that she could muster to approach
Gavin in the first place and ask him to be her partner. He
did not even have the decency to cancel in person or even
call. No, he sent a text message.

She was gutted; the devastation was so much that she
did not want to attend the event herself.

"I'm not going anymore," she cried and proclaimed
into her pillow.

"Oh, no you don't. You will go, even if I have to drag
you there by your hair," her mom roared angrily. "We
paid a fortune for that dress, who cares if that boy doesn't
want to go anymore?"

"Honey, it's your special night. It doesn't matter if you go with a partner or alone," her father encouraged.

In the end, her mother asked her friend's son to go with her and to her surprise; she thoroughly enjoyed the evening, all the girls swooning over her handsome partner.

She smiled, thinking how she took advantage of her disappointment and her parents' desperation to have her attend what they called a right of passage by demanding to go to the after party. She was never allowed to attend parties or have sleepovers or even go out on dates. So it was a real feat that she was able to attend the after party.

Her excitement soon turned to disappointment, when by the end of practise, Roger did not show up. She was distracted during the entire session, conceding three goals. She chastised herself for being a lousy goalie, her mood taking a nosedive with each passing second

"Don't worry Sasha, must be the bump on your head," Suzy commented.

Sasha immediately touched her forehead, "'n doempie?"

"Is nie so bad nie, is nie 'n doempie nie," Stacy chimed in.

Maybe it was better that Roger never showed up. "Imagine, doempie doempie dom kop," she whispered under her breath as she walked to the parking lot, to where her father was already waiting for her.

5

Life seemed to go back to normal afterward and Sasha, fell right back into her normal routine, counting down the days until the results would be published in the newspaper. She looked forward to the beginning of the rest of her life. She always heard people say, that life gets easier after high school. She needed to find a job because studying was not an option; her parents had told her that due to financial constraints that they were unable to pay for studies.

She was disappointed but accepted it gracefully. She was so used to things always going wrong for her, all part of the same cosmic joke.

She took it all in stride. Instead of looking forward to the next time she would see Roger, she focussed on all the things she had control over.

Afternoons alone at home were her favourite. While cleaning she danced around with the broom, the music blaring loudly over the speakers. Dressed in shorts, a tank top, barefoot, hair in a messy bun, she spun around the room, gleeful to have the space to herself.

While taking the trash out, she stopped-dead in her tracks when Roger pulled up to the curb in his blue Corsa. For a second, Sasha stood stoned face clutching the black bag in her hand, eyes wide staring at Roger getting out of the car.

He smiled, "Hi Sash."

"Roger?"

Walking over to the gate he asked, "Can I come in?"

"Uhm," Sasha stood awkwardly and nodded, unable to find her voice.

"How's your head?" He asked looking at the purplish-blue mark above her eyebrow.

"It's fine," she answered slowly and discarded the bag into the big rolling bin outside. She wiped her hands on her shorts. "Why are you here?"

Roger smiled cockily, "I wanted to see if you are okay."

"Why?" she asked stupidly. They were both still standing awkwardly facing each other. "Sorry, you want to come inside, I was just busy cleaning." She gestured toward the front door.

"Sure."

"Can I get you some juice, tea, coffee?"

"No thank you, I'm fine," he waved her off and followed her leisurely into the kitchen, where Sasha quickly replaced the black bag in the bin, washed her hands in the sink, and walked back to the living room, Roger following her all the while.

"You have pretty feet," he commented taking a seat on the sofa.

"Huh?" Sasha blushed and quickly hid her feet under the pillow on the opposite sofa.

"Don't hide them," Roger laughed.

"Nee, is jy mal. Hoekom kyk jy my voete?"

24

"Jy sal verbaas wees, hoeveel meisies loop rond met Nik-Nak tone hier buite."

They both laughed.

"So why the unexpected visit?"

"I enjoyed chatting with you the other night," he said matter-of-factly.

"Why now?" she asked incredulously.

"Honestly?"

"Yes, please."

"Well, I didn't know how approachable you were." He started explaining, looking down before continuing, "jy lyk altyd so lyk jy sal 'n mens afswitch."

Sasha's mouth fell open and then laughed, "What? You are not serious."

"Oh, I couldn't be anymore serious and besides, your dad scares the crap out of me," Roger tagged on.

"Oh, he's a marshmallow," she giggled, "once you get to know him."

They chatted for a while and after he left Sasha was floating on a cloud. For the first time, she felt pretty. Not that Roger asked her out or anything like that. It felt good knowing that guys thought of approaching her, even if she had a face that scared them off.

6

The visits became more frequent, chats longer, leaving Sasha to build castles in the sky. Their results were scheduled to be published at 12 o'clock the following evening and as luck would have it, Roger offered to drive Sasha to the Mall to wait for the arrival of the newspapers, together with the rest of their class.

Her parents were becoming a little suspicious with his constant presence, but raised no questions.

"So Roger, what are your plans for the future?" Mr. Peters inquired as they sat in the lounge on the blue floral print couches, while Sasha set up the oak coffee table for an informal dinner. It was a warm December night, the breeze blowing in through the open windows, fanning Sasha's hair across her forehead as she covered the table with a tablecloth; before leaving Roger and her father to their conversation.

Roger cleared his throat, "I will be starting a toolmaker's apprenticeship in January, Sir."

Sasha entered the room once more with the smell of cheese and herbs wafting around her, as she placed the casserole dish on the placemat. Mrs. Peters came in carrying a fresh green summer salad as an accompaniment to the beef lasagne, taking a seat next to Sasha on the loveseat.

"That looks wonderful love," her father complimented before focussing on Roger again, "that's a great opportunity."

"Yes, Sir," he shot a glance at Sasha, who sat looking from her father to Roger.

"Well, let's eat," her mother declared and leaned forward to dish for her husband. They proceeded to eat their dinner and making small talk, refining their plans for the following evening.

Sasha woke up excited and nervous, she knew she had studied, that she would probably pass but the anxiety over waiting for the results, the possible embarrassment of failing and not seeing your name in print, had her muscles in a twist and her stomach in a tight ball. She wanted to call Roger and cancel, opting to rather face the inevitability alone, but as she picked up her phone from the little black side table, it rang. It startled her, spying the time before answering the call from the unknown number.

She wondered who would be calling her before 6 o'clock in the morning, "hello?"

She heard her aunt's excitement over the receiver before she could even make out who she was talking to, "congrats Sasha," she screamed into the phone.

"Aunty Becca?" Sasha asked confused, sitting straight up in her bed.

"You passed," the response came.

"What?"

"You passed, I am so proud of you," Aunt Becca gushed.

"But," Sasha stuttered incoherently, "but, the results are only suppose to come out tonight?"

"No, it came out at 12 o'clock already."

"Really?" she asked shocked, brushing back the hair from her face, "did I really pass?"

"Yes, I am looking at your name in the paper as we speak."

Sasha screamed from the bottled up excitement, jumping around in her pyjamas, "thank you, Aunty Becca. I have to go; I need to get a newspaper."

"Oh okay, okay congratulations."

"Thank you," Sasha ended the call and hugged her phone to her chest, jumping around the room.

She dressed hastily, tripping over her pants, hopping from side to side with her phone clutched to her face between her cheek and shoulder, "The results are out."

Stacy screamed half asleep, "What? No, that's tonight."

"No, it was released last night or this morning or whatever," Sasha waved her hand dismissively, "my aunt just called and told me, I passed."

"Nooooo!" Stacy screamed and jumped out of bed, "we need to get a paper."

"Yes, get dressed I'll pick you up in 5 minutes, my mom said I can use her car."

"Okay, okay, shit Sasha, is it real? I'm so nervous."

"Me too, I have to see it myself, it doesn't feel real yet." Sasha confessed nervously. "See you in a few," Sasha said and ended the call.

Sasha hooted in front of Stacy's mother's house, tapping her fingers impatiently on the steering wheel. Stacy came bounding out of the house, "Hey Sasha, eeek!" She squealed as she climbed into the passenger seat.

"Hey Stace, where do you think we'll find a paper," she glanced at her wristwatch, "it's only almost 7 o'clock?"

"I'm not sure, we can try all the shops, I guess," Stacy mused and asked, "Hey did you call Roger? You guys have been spending quite a bit of time together."

Sasha felt heat flush her cheeks, so she looked out of the side window and answered, "no I haven't, you think I should?'

"Sure, why not? He was going to go to the mall with us tonight, wasn't he?"

"Okay, let me quickly call him and tell him." She retrieved her cell phone from her pocket and dialled his number.

He answered groggily, "hello."

"Roger?"

"Yes, Sasha?"

"I'm sorry, I'm calling, uhm, the results are out."

"What?" She heard his voice raise an octave before clearing his throat, "are you sure?"

"Yes, my aunt called me and told me, I just picked up Stacy, we're going to go look for a shop that's open already."

"oh, okay. Swing by, I'll go with you guys."

"Okay, we'll be there in a minute."

"See you just now," Sasha said and smiled at Stacy ending the call. "We have to pick him up, okay?"

Stacy did not respond, she just gave Sasha a sly look and nodded.

Roger was standing outside waiting for them when they pulled up to the curb. Sasha stopped the car, Roger got into the back seat, "Morning Stacy, Sasha."

"Morning," Sasha responded.

"Hi," Stacy greeted, glancing over her shoulder.

"Can you guys believe this is really the beginning of the end?" Roger asked.

Sasha looked at him in the rear-view mirror. He seemed tense, staring through the window, watching the houses pass. His jaw taut, accentuating his high cheekbones, his perfectly shaped lips, and dark brown eyes. He was clutching his hands in his lap; it was the first time she ever saw him so unsure, so lacking in confidence. It made him seem more human to her and not like the angelic being she always imagined him to be.

The first store they stopped at was closed, so they tried another. The parking lot was filled with cars and students loitering waiting for the shop to open, the store-owner arrived at the same time as Sasha. The excitement and anxiety multiplied with each step they got closer to discovering their fate.

They each purchased newspapers and had it sprawled out on the floor in the parking lot, anxiously looking for their names. For a few minutes, there was silence before one by one they located their names and the cheers erupted, breaking through the silence. News papers were flying in the air as they embraced, laughed, some even cried. Sasha stood staring at everyone, as if disconnected from her body. She watched herself from the outside as if she was having an out of body experience, happy that she passed but sad that it was the end of an era of her life. It scared her to think of what would come next. She had no idea what to expect. She was still contemplating when all too soon, she felt arms around her, Roger embraced her, lifting her in his strong arms, swinging her around. Their gazes locked, she saw the excitement in his eyes like two dark pools of joy.

It was the first time she aligned the dark with joy. It was quite a revelation. He put her down, not breaking their focus on each other, slowly bent his head hovering just a few centimetres from her face, searching her eyes and then plunged his lips to hers in a kiss.

Sasha felt heat spread down through her body from her lips. Her body instinctively responded as she wrapped her arms around his neck and deepened the kiss. In that moment they were the only ones who existed and all else seized.

She was still floating when he drove her home. Stacy opted to stay with the rest of the crowd to celebrate, but Sasha knew she had to return her mom's car before all hell broke loose. Pulling up on the drive way, Sasha opened the gate for Roger to park the car, when her mother came out of the house, a drying cloth in her hands.

Sasha excitedly walked over to where her mother stood, Roger followed close behind her.

"We passed Ma," she declared nervously, the look in her mother's eyes warning her to not push it.

"Morning Roger, congratulations on passing."

"Thank you Mrs. Peters, I am beyond excited," Roger said smiling and shot a glance to Sasha, who was standing fidgeting looking at the ground.

"Your parents will be very happy."

"Speaking of which, I have to get home. Spread the news of unemployment to my parents," Roger joked, turned to Sasha, "I'll call you later."

"Okay, laters." She watched him turn and leave, her mother still standing by quietly.

"Bye Roger," her mother said and turned her focus to Sasha, "What?"

Sasha smiled feebly, "do you want to see the newspaper mom?"

Her mother nodded while Sasha paged through the paper and pointed out her name.

"You didn't get an exemption?" Her mother asked.

"No, I, uhm, I have to get my results from the school later," Sasha answered deflated.

"If you are waiting for me to congratulate you, you are going to wait for a long time. You could have done better."

Her mother's words slapped her in the face; the searing pain reverberated through her body, slashing at her heart. She bowed her head, diverting her eyes from her mother and walked into the house, quietly closing the bedroom door behind her. She stood against it, hugging her arms around her body. Trying to hold herself together, she touched her lips, kissing Roger felt like a lifetime ago.

Before doing the only thing she could, she cried lying on her bed as she heard her mom leave, yelling from the doorway, "I'm leaving, I'll be back later."

7

Roger arrived later that afternoon, finding Sasha in the front yard, lying on a checker-blanket on the grass. Her hair flailed above her head. He stood by the gate watching her, her bare legs slightly glistening in the sunlight. She was so lost in thought; she did not even notice his presence.

After a few minutes he whistled drawing her attention to him. She looked over to him and was startled when she saw him leaning over the gate watching her. Heat flooded her face turning her cheeks beet red.

"Hi," she greeted and cringed at the anticlimactic greeting.

He smiled, "hi," opened the gate and walked over to where she was now sitting looking down, trying to hide her feet, and took a seat next to her on the blanket. He lifted her chin with his index finger, so that their focus met and whispered softly, "hi."

She smiled shyly and greeted again under her breath, "hi."

"Why are you lying outside?" He asked curiously.

She lied back down, "I needed to feel free."

"Free?"

"Don't worry about it; I enjoy lying on the grass and watching the grass," she responded enjoying the heat of the sun on her face.

Roger leaned back onto his elbows on the blanket and started running his fingers through her hair sprawled out above her head on the blanket. She loved the feel of his fingers in her hair, it was calming and brought back vague memories of when she was younger and her mother would do the same.

"So?" She asked uncertain focussing on Roger, trying to avoid where her mind was going.

He laughed, "so what?"

Sasha rolled her eyes and threw her arm over her eyes.

"Oh come on, I'm playing with you." He waited for her to open her eyes before continuing, "You're talking about the kiss?" He asked with a smirk.

She did not answer but her stare was screaming for an explanation.

"I've wanted to do that for a long time and this morning just seemed like the best time," now it was his turn to look uncertain. "I liked kissing you; I would like to do it again, if you will allow it?"

"Really?" The question was out of her mouth before she could stop it.

"Yes, really. Didn't you?" He turned it back on her.

She looked at him dumbstruck before answering, "I liked it a lot," she said and blushed.

He looked at her intensely, bent down and softly kissed her lips for the second time that day.

She touched her lips and asked, "What does this mean?"

"Well, if you like I can, hoe se mens, ek vra die antwoord," and laughed a little.

36

Sasha burst out in a fit of giggles, "You ask that if it was 1960."

He joined in the laugher, "1960 or not, I'm serious. What do you say?"

"I've never had a boyfriend before," she answered honestly.

"That doesn't matter, I've enjoyed the time we've spent together and I like you, well I more than like you. What do you say?"

"Okay," She answered softly but excitedly.

"Do I still have to ask you're parents' permission, you think?" He asked sincerely.

Sasha's excitement was quickly sobered and replaced by fear, "uhm, I don't know, do we have to?"

"Geez Sash, we are finished with school and I would like to take you out sometime as well. Don't you want anybody to know?"

"I guess I do, I just don't know what they will say," her mother's reaction from that morning ran through her mind as a shudder ran over her body but she quickly suppressed it, put a smile on her face as Roger took her hand in his.

"Don't worry, I'm good with parents," he smiled his crooked smile as reassurance.

"If you say so, I might as well enjoy the knowledge of having a boyfriend before my father kills you," she joked as he pulled her close to him in a reassuring hug.

8

S asha fidgeted all afternoon, biting her nails, giggling whenever she thought of Roger and the kisses they had shared. Touching her lips almost as if it were all a dream. She couldn't wait for the next time she would get to see him.

Her mother arrived home later that day, in better spirits and started preparing dinner. Sasha helped where she could but mostly stayed out of her mother's way. She had decided to put the conversation they had the morning out of her mind, just like she had on many other occasions. She accepted that that was just the way her mother was and that it was technically her fault, for not studying hard enough. Not that it mattered because there were no funds for her to study. She had to find a job and the prospect of having Roger in her life was making all the bad seem less daunting.

Her father congratulated her on passing when he arrived home from work and when Roger arrived just after dinner around 7 o'clock; he shook Roger's hand and wished him luck for the future. There was a flutter in her stomach as she watched the exchange between them, her eyes never diverting from Roger's face. He smiled at her and took a seat next to her casually as he had many times before. They were seated in the lounge, Mr. Peters in the armchair, Mrs. Peters on the sofa facing the television set, while Roger and Sasha sat awkwardly on the loveseat, Sasha's nerves almost making her bounce.

Roger cleared his throat, "Mr. Peters, Mrs. Peters."

All eyes turned to him, Sasha's face went white the blood draining from her it as she turned her gaze on Roger, "now?" She asked softly, nobody else heard except Rogerr.

He smiled reassuringly at her, taking her hand in his. Alarmed she pulled her hand away from his and immediately looked from him to her father and lastly her mother.

"Yes," Mr. Peters said.

"Well, I know this might be old fashioned but I really like Sasha and I wanted your permission to date her?"

It was silent, you could hear a pin drop, Sasha was holding her breath awaiting their response.

Her father looked from Roger to Sasha, but she refused to meet his gaze; steadfastly focussing on her hands.

"We appreciate you asking our permission and I guess we cannot object, because if we did, then you would probably just go ahead behind our backs," Mr. Peters started explaining casting a sideways glance to his wife before continuing, "if this is what you and Sasha want then we will not stand in your way."

"Thank you Mr. Peters," Roger said sincerely.

"Thanks dad," Sasha said releasing her long held breath. She looked to her mother, who still sat silently.

They had a lovely evening further talking about the following year, Roger's apprenticeship, Sasha's plan for finding a job and by the end of the evening when Roger left, Sasha walked him out, her parents still sitting in the lounge. As soon as she closed the door behind them, she turned to Roger slowly, smiling radiantly.

"You are crazy;" she joked admiringly, "I never in a million years thought that would go that easy." She clasped her hands in front of her chest elated.

"I told you I am good with parents," he took a step forward, closing the distance between them and wrapped his arms around her waist, kissing her tenderly.

"Who knew my life would change so much in just one day?" Sasha mused, "I am officially unemployed and now I have a boyfriend."

"I like the way that sounds," Roger said and let go of her quickly, taking a step back as the front door swung open.

"Sasha, it's getting late," Mr. Peters said.

"Okay Dad, I'll be right in."

"Good night Mr. Peters," Roger said and then looked down at Sasha, "Good night, Sash. See you tomorrow."

Her eyes glowed with pride, "Good night Roger," she said formally smiling and turned around heading back into the house, watching Roger leave before closing the door.

Her parents were already in their bedroom, so after locking up she rushed to her bedroom. Stripping off her clothes and changing into her pyjamas, getting into bed with her phone clutched in her hand. She could not get the smile off her face. The door to her bedroom opened just as a message pinged on her phone. Sasha put the phone under her pillow without reading the message and diverted her attention to the door. Her mother peeked in, "Are you sleeping?"

"No mom, I just got in bed now."

"So, is this why Roger's been hanging out here all this time?"

"No," she responded shocked and sat up in her bed.

"Maybe you would have done better in school," she waved her hand about, "as jou kop nie so vol muis neste was nie."

"Ma, ek het nog nooit 'n boyfriend gehad nie en ek het nie geweet Roger like my nie," she looked down hurt and continued, "he just asked me today."

"Wel as jy voel jy is jags dan beter jy sien laat jy clinic toe gaan."

Sasha looked up shocked as her mother turned to leave, a lone tear gliding over her cheek. She never expected that, in her mind she always imagined the day that the need would arise for the birds and bees talk, she never quite pictured it like this. She was left more confused, with so many questions, with the realisation that she would never be able to talk to her mother and that she would need to learn these things on her own.

Retrieving her phone from under the pillow, she checked her messages.

Hi Baby, I'm home and I miss you already. I can't believe you said yes and that you are officially mine. Sweet dreams. Call you in the morning.

She hit the reply button,

Happy you are home safely. You have made me very happy today. Dream of me.
Xoxoxo S

She hugged her phone again, smiled through her tears, and drifted off into a peaceful sleep.

9

For the first time in Sasha's life, she woke up happy, happier than she could ever have imagined she could be. It did not bother her that her mother was so cavalier about well, everything. She decided to be happy; she decided that it would be a good day. She had so much to be grateful for, yet fear was her constant companion, her fear of being inadequate. Experience has taught her that there were always dark clouds just beyond the sunlight. The constant cosmic joke the universe played on her was just an unavoidable factor in her life that she had long since accepted, put a smile on her face and tried to sing through the rain or rather thunderstorms in her case.

Her relationship with Roger blossomed; they spent all their spare time together. He played with her hair; and without fail it reminded her of when she was younger just after her hair started growing, when her mother used to run her fingers through the strands. They held hands, took long walks, watched movies, shared ice creams, and when Roger started his apprenticeship, they text each other relentlessly throughout the day until they saw each other at night.

The fear she felt over the relationship, slowly started to ebb the more time they spent together, she was glowing and becoming more confident with each passing day. Roger seemed to be drawing the best out of her.

It took her a little over three months to find a job, it was a temporary assignment but she was happy none the less, it was all a new adventure.

The year sped by with Sasha being offered a permanent position at the same company and loving every minute of it. It was a normal administrative position but she enjoyed it, she even started saving some of her meagre funds towards a car.

After two years, they were still going strong. She spent every free second she had with Roger, abandoning the friends she made when she was at school, completely absorbed by the love they shared. He became her everything, she did not even recognise or acknowledge other guys even though she was getting the eye from guys at work. She had finally found her place in her world.

"You know I love you, right?" Roger whispered in her ear as they were lying on his bed making out.

"Of course," she responded with closed eyes, knotting her hands in his hair.

He trailed kisses down her neck, lightly tracing her collarbone with his fingers before cupping her breasts. Gently lifting her shirt and placed soft kisses over her stomach. Sasha tensed as he moved down; he sensed it and lifted his head, looking her straight in the eyes, "are you okay?"

"Yes, sorry," she apologised nervously.

"Do you want me to stop?"

"I don't know," fear the predominant feature on her face.

"We don't have to, if you aren't ready."

"I think. I think, I'm ready."

Shock washed over Roger's face, "are you sure?" They have been at this same juncture so many times before.

"Yes, uhm, but I'm scared."

"We can take it slow."

That was the day Sasha finally gave herself, her body, to Roger. She surrendered her will by giving him the only gift she could, to express her level of commitment, she wanted to give herself to him in every possible way.

"I love you," She whispered lying in his arms, spent.

"I love you too. Are you okay?" Roger asked kissing her on the head as he traced patterns on her back.

"I'm fine," she answered unsure of how much details she should divulge.

"I didn't hurt you, did I?"

"No, I mean. It was sore but,"

"but, what?" He asked concerned.

"It was weird," she confessed.

"Weird good or weird bad?"

"Good," she smiled shyly, "I liked being that close to you." She blushed as if confessing to a crime. "I wouldn't mind doing that again."

"You have no idea," he smiled hugging her tighter and kissing her head.

"Will it hurt every time?"

"No, it won't," he answered sincerely and smiled.

Sasha stood in front of the mirror in her room, examining herself. She felt different and yet everything looked the same. She laughed thinking that she obviously

looks the same, "what do you expect? Horns." She
laughed at her absurd musings.

For the first time in years she sat down at her desk,
picked up her journal and started writing.

*The last time I wrote, I felt silly. Now I am writing and
not addressing it to anybody because I need an outlet or
else I will explode. I have nobody to talk to, apart from
Roger but I can't say these things to him, can I?*

*I gave myself to him today and it was amazing, weird
but amazing. I was scared, but fear is my default setting.
Now having experienced it, I wonder what I was so scared
of. I want to do it again.* She smiled sheepishly.

*It was embarrassing when I had to use Roger's t-shirt
to wipe the blood off.* She cupped her face in her hands,
the pen sticking out through her fingers, embarrassed. *It's
completely ruined. I'll probably have to replace it, even
though he reassured me that I don't have to. I want to.*

*I guess, having sex with the person you love does make
it special, though it was my first time; I have nothing to
compare it to. Knowing that he loves me means
everything.*

*My mom keeps complaining that I spend too much time
with Roger. That's not true; I spend time with my friends
at work.*

Sasha felt like a weight was lifted off her shoulders
having written her confession. She pushed herself back
from the desk and quickly ran to the kitchen in search of a
lighter and when she returned to her room, she crumpled
the paper in her hand, placed it in the steel waste bin
under the desk and lit it. She watched the flames burn over
the paper devouring her confession and smiled, seeing the

paper turn black where the flames licked, it made her feel free.

10

For the next few months, life was bliss. Sasha and Roger made love as often as they could, sometime even in the back seat of his car or the front seat, wherever the mood hit. Sasha became more aware of her sexuality and the affect her body had on him. She felt beautiful when he looked at her naked body, completely comfortable around him and comfortable in her own skin.

But by the time their third year anniversary was approaching, things changed subtle things at first. Roger had made a boat-load of new friends at the company he worked for, and spent more time with them devoting less time to Sasha. He became more possessive and demanding over her, accusing her of cheating on him occasionally, when she attended a work function or visited family on the weekends with her parents.

She kept reassuring him of her loyalty and her love, consoling herself that he cared for her dearly and that that was why he behaved this way, because despite the changes, their love making was still fiery, whenever they did get time alone, which was few and far between now. But still, she loved him.

He insisted that she stay at home most of the time, while he was out with friends. She did not really care; she never went anywhere, so accustomed to not being allowed to go anywhere, first from her parents growing up and now Roger - All in the name of love.

"Hi babe," Sasha answered her phone excitedly when she saw Roger's name on her cell phone screen.

"Sasha," he sounded frantic and panicked.

Her stomach dropped, fear screaming in her ears, "What's wrong?" she heard his engine roar in the background.

"I'm almost there by you, come outside," he answered hurriedly.

"What happened?" she felt her throat thicken and tears threaten but held it back. Checked the time on her phone, it was already 10 o'clock, and walked briskly to the front door.

Her father peeked through the bedroom door, "where's the fire?"

She was startled, "Roger's outside."

"This time of the night?"

"Yeah, he just called and said I must quickly come outside." She turned around and headed outside, Roger pulled up to the curb as soon as she opened the door. She ended the call and felt relief wash over her, as her focus ran over his profile in the car.

Roger raised his hand in greeting, "Mr. Peters."

Sasha turned around and saw her father standing by the door who directed asked, "What's wrong Roger?"

"Sorry for coming around so late Sir, I seemed to have misplaced my wallet," he explains and cast a glance to Sasha.

"Oh, okay," Mr. Peter says looking from Roger to Sasha and then walked back into the house, leaving the door ajar.

"You lost your wallet?" Sasha asked perplexed. "I was so worried; I thought you got hurt or something."

"Sorry, did you see it? Did I forget it here by you?"

"You left over an hour ago, where were you?" She asked confused.

"I was at the club with the guys," he said rolling his eyes, annoyed at the question.

"I thought you were going home, you were in such a rush to leave."

He stood looking at her and brushed his hand over his head, "the guys were waiting for me, that's why I left."

She felt hurt, "So is that why you always leave early?"

"God Sasha, you can't be out late, you don't do clubs, I am young, I have friends. I don't need your permission."

"I never said you need permission," she retorted defiantly and folded her arms over her torso.

"Will you help me find my wallet or not?"

She walked past him to the car, opened the driver's side door, looked in the cabby, on the back seat, and in the crevices by the doors while Roger looked in the boot.

"Here," she proclaimed after feeling around on the floor by the pedals.

"You found it?"

"Yes."

"Where was it?"

"On the floor."

He put the wallet in his jean's pocket," gently pulled Sasha out of the car, "thank you," grateful that she found it.

"Pleasure," she answered and wrapped her arms around him in an embrace.

"I have to go," he said placing a kiss on her forehead.

"Where?"

"Don't start Sasha," he became annoyed once more.

"What do you mean, don't start? Can I not ask a question?" She took a step back from him, furious.

"Look, I'll call you tomorrow, the guys,"

She cut him off mid-sentence, "the guys? Seriously? You spend so much time with them, more than you spend with me lately and that's all I get?" Her voice was shaky with unshed tears.

He drew closer to her, kissed her cheek, got into the car and said, "Good night Sasha, I will not take part in the fight you obviously want to start." Started the engine and added, "Call you tomorrow."

He drove off, while Sasha stood staring after him shocked.

Back in her room, she stood under her ceiling lamp at her duvet, confused, she had no idea what just happened. What was with these late night clubbing sprees that she had no knowledge of and boy did Roger's attitude stink.

11

S he did not see Roger the following day, tried calling him but his phone kept sending her to voicemail.

Hey Baby,
Been trying to call you. Call me. Love you
Xoxox S

No response…

Sasha tried keeping busy, reading, watching television, even washing her sneakers, but nothing could keep her mind from wandering back to Roger. The conversation, argument or as Roger referred to it, the fight that she wanted to start, replayed in her mind. She thought over the entire span of their relationship, the good, the bad and the suddenly ugly. Was it her fault, it had to be, right? What other explanation could there be?

Maybe he was bored with her; she was so boring after all, she thought. Never allowed to go clubbing, not that it even interested her to begin with. But assuming responsibility was her go-to-move.

She decided that nothing really mattered because she loved him and they would just clear the air when he called.

In lieu of this she sent him another text after her bath before getting in bed that night:

Hi Babe, I hope you had a good day. Sorry about last night. I miss you. Will I see you tomorrow? Love you Xoxoxox S

She laid in bed staring at her phone in the dark. A message pinged just as she placed it on the nightstand next to the bed. She hastily grabbed it,

Hey baby, sorry I forgot to charge my phone. Missed you too. I'll swing by after work. Love you.

Relief spread through her body like a warm cup of Milo on a cold winter's night.

12

Sasha fell back into her regular routine, pushing all her fears about her relationship aside. It gnawed on her that they were not spending a lot of time together and when they happened to be together, they either fought or made love. There was no middle ground. The fights got worse with each passing day, growing in intensity. The more they fought, the more Sasha retreated into herself. She still wore a smile on her face, but deep down she felt lost.

"Hey Micky, can I ask you something?" Sasha turned her chair to face Micky, working at the desk next to her.

"Yeah, what's up?" Micky asked with his deep baritone, turning towards her.

"What does it mean, if a guy no longer makes an effort to spend time with you?"

Micky sat back in his chair, before answering, "it depends."

"On what?" For the first time in over two years she noticed how handsome her colleague was; perfectly dressed in a crisp white shirt, tailored black pants and spotless shoes. It startled her to realise that she noticed his looks. Shaking her head to clear her thoughts she concentrated on what Micky was saying, "What's his reason for not making time for you?"

"Well, maybe it's my fault." She shrugged and continued, "I don't do clubbing, I don't go to parties etc. I am pretty boring," she laughed without humour.

"So you think it's your fault? Tell me, do you want to be alone or do you want him to spend time with you, doing things that you like doing?"

"Of course I want him to spend time with me, but can I really expect him to always just sit around at home with me?"

"If he loves you, he would want to spend time with you, even if it meant doing nothing."

Micky's answer rocked Sasha, it felt like cold water was poured over her body, flowing from her head right down to her toes.

"If he loved me," she whispered breathlessly, looking down at the ugly blue carpets in the office.

"I'm sorry, Sasha. That was harsh to say," Micky quickly said vacating his seat. His close proximity gave her a skrik when he suddenly laid his hand on her shoulder and said, "Look, it's not always the case. Speak to him; it might just be a misunderstanding."

"We barely talk anymore, everything ends in a fight," she confessed and closed her eyes, resting her head in her hands.

"I hope you guys work things out, I'm sorry for my callous response."

"No," she said plastering a smile on her face, "I asked, I appreciate your candour."

They went back to work, but spoke more often and even went out for lunch together on different occasions.

He was a very good friend, she found herself opening up to him a little.

13

G ood lord, things went from bad to worse…

Sasha's cousins passed stories on to her about how Roger was cheating on her. Stories of him hanging out with Stacy floated around the township. The more she heard, the more she hid. She hid from her family, avoided everyone who could possibly give her any more bad news. She isolated herself, like a caterpillar in a cocoon. Afraid to hear any more, afraid that she might believe everything; swimming in a sea of denial.

The fear that she worked so hard to keep under control was slowing seeping back into her body, her soul. She felt like a dark hole was sucking the life right out of her.

"Where's Roger, didn't you say he would be joining us for the potjie?" Sasha's father asked happily while he made a fire; dressed in a shorts, t-shirt and apron.

It was a beautiful summer's day; even Sasha's mother was in a good mood.

"Yes, he said he would come. He's probably still at home," Sasha said looking at her phone again.

After lounging around the pool, swimming, soaking up the sun for more than three hours, she decided to call Roger one last time.

"Where are you?" She asked as soon as he answered the call. She heard laughter and music in the background.

"I'll come around later," he answered with laughter in his voice. "shhhhh," he said away from the phone.

"Where are you? You said you would join us."

"Sasha don't nag please, I said I'll come around later."

"I'm not nagging, you said."

He interrupted her then, "fine, I'm not coming," he declared angrily.

"What?"

"Yes, you heard me."

"Seriously Roger?" She asked shocked and heard a female voice in the background.

"I have to go," he interjected quickly and cut the call before Sasha could say anything.

She stared at her phone like an idiot for a few minutes, letting the exchange she just had with Roger sink in.

She could not cry in front of her family, she had to rein it in and wait for the evening when she retired to her bedroom, where she gave in to the pain she felt searing through her chest all afternoon. True to his word, Roger never showed up.

In the quiet confinement of her room, she scrolled through her contacts, hid her caller id and hit the call button, biting her nails as she waited for the answer.

"Hello," came the answer.

"Hi Stacy," Sasha greeted nervously. She heard music in the background, she could almost swear it was the same music she heard when she called Roger the afternoon, but *that was silly*, she thought. Everybody listened to music.

"Shhhhhh… Sasha, why is your number hidden?"

"Oh, I don't know," she lied.

"What's up?" Stacy asked casually.

"Stacy, I know this might sound crazy but I am driving myself crazy wondering and I just have to ask," she struggled for words and continued taking a deep breath, "are you and uhm, are you and Roger?" She tried but could not get the words to exit her mouth.

"What? Seriously, are you calling me to ask me shit like this? Accusing me?"

"I'm sorry, I just needed to know."

"Sasha, I don't have time for this." She spat the words angrily and ended the call.

It dawned on Sasha that Stacy did not confirm nor did she deny the accusation and that realisation hurt. She tried suppressing the pain, happily drowning herself in denial once more, clinging to the past, happy memories and the delusion that Roger would never hurt her.

14

"Why the hell did you call Stacy?" Roger's voice roared into the receiver as Sasha answered the call.

"What?" Sasha answered hoarse from all the crying.

"What the hell is wrong with you?" He raised his voice, it was dripping with disdain.

"Why are you yelling at me? What's the time?" She rubbed her eyes disorientated.

"For fuck's sake Sasha, are you going to call every girl I've ever slept with because of your insecurities?"

Tears pooled in her eyes, "I called Stacy, I just, I just."

"You just what? You think you can rain on my parade, you are not my fucken mother."

"Stop swearing at me," she stuttered. "I never claimed to be your mother, Roger. Wait, wait a minute,"

"Don't tell me to wait, you have crossed the line," he said through clenched jaws.

"You said all the girls? So is it true, you slept with Stacy?"

"Don't put words in my mouth."

"I didn't put any words in your mouth, you said."

He interrupted her once more, "yes, so since you want to throw my words back at me, listen carefully to what I say. We are done; I am tired of your accusations, insecurities, and everything. It's over."

"Roger?" Sasha's voice cracked as the tears rolled uncontrolled over her cheeks.

"Don't. Goodbye Sasha," he said with finality and ended the call.

The silence stretched as Sasha sat upright in bed staring into the abyss, clutching the duvet to her mouth, muffling the sounds of her cries. Her heart, in fact her whole body ached, she had never felt this much pain in her life, it will surely kill her, she thought. How had everything spiralled out of control so rapidly?

Sasha trudged around like a Zombi, lifeless and empty for the next couple of months. She had built her whole world around Roger and now that world was destroyed.

I am damaged! The pain of losing you is all consuming. I feel empty. You left me alone, when all I ever had was you, there are no friends I could turn to, to try and forget you. Everything reminds me of you, even my body; I cannot look at myself in the mirror, all I see is a gigantic hole. I have to plaster a smile on my face when I am in public, even though I cry myself to sleep and wake up every morning with tears hovering in my eyes. I talk through a closed throat, swallowing thickly, suppressing the urge to run, hide and cry because the urge of falling apart is much stronger than I am. Losing you meant losing me and the pain is too much to bear. I wish I could hate your guts, despise your existence and rewind back to a time before you existed for me, but I love you too much. You opened my mind, my heart and my soul by giving me love but took that same love and destroyed my being and cast the pieces into the depths of oblivion...

15

"Hi Sasha," she heard the greeting coming from behind her as she opened the gate, when she arrived home from work. She spun around startled. She was about to greet, an automatic response but the wind was knocked out of her, when low and behold Roger stood looking at her with his hands in his pockets.

"Roger?" her voice broke as she said his name, she cleared her throat, "what are you doing here?"

He smiled, "I wanted to see how you were doing?"

"Why?"

"Come on Sash, I care about you," he answered and took a step closer to her.

She instinctively moved back, "it's been two months, not one phone call, nothing." she wrapped her arms around her body, trying to hold her body together. She could feel herself slip; she couldn't let the sight of him affect her like this, his voice felt like a warm caress.

"We both needed time to cool off," he said waving his hand in the air.

"Time to cool off?" She asked confused.

"Can I come inside?"

Only then did she realise they were still standing outside. "Where's your car?"

"Oh I felt like taking a walk."

She turned around, opened the gate and entered the yard without another word. He followed after her silently. She unlocked the door and clicked the lights on, "Mommy, Daddy?" She called but there was no response.

"I'll be right back, going to put my bag my room," she told Roger as he made himself comfortable in the lounge.

Walking briskly to her room, she placed her bag on the desk and slipped off her shoes. She sat on the edge of the bed and took a deep breath, shutting her eyes pinching the bridge of her nose. She knew that seeing him would cause the pain to start anew.

"Sasha," Roger whispered, standing in front of her. "Are you okay?" Sasha's eyelashes flew open and she stared at him wordlessly. He took a step closer to her and ignored when she pulled back a little hugging herself tightly. He gently tugged her right arm and pulled her up so that their bodies were flush against each other.

"Roger, no," she said under her breath, tears threatening at the corners of her eyes.

"Sasha," he whispered softly, brushing his index finger over her cheek, wiping off the tear that escaped. Bent down and kissed her cheek before moving to her lips.

She pushed him away but his strong arms constricted her movement, "please don't," she begged.

"Why not?" He asked and placed another soft kiss on her cheek.

"You left me," she whimpered.

"I am here now, don't fight me," and crushed his mouth to hers, coaxing it open.

She silently wrestled with herself, trying desperately not to give in to his advances. He had yet to offer an explanation and yet, feeling the warmth of his body pressed against her, the strength of his arms wrapped around her, the hunger in his kisses, chipped away at her resolve until nothing mattered, giving in to her desire to feel whole. She released her long held breath and he took advantage, kissing her hungrily as she let down her guard, surrendering her defences and giving herself to him.

16

"What does this mean?" She sat wrapped in her bed sheets, watching Roger jump around the room from one leg to the other getting dressed.

"Get dressed before your parents get back," he avoided the question, sat down on the bed and tied his shoe laces.

She begrudgingly got out of bed and got dressed, "you didn't answer me."

"I don't know," he sat with his hands steepled looking at the floor.

"You've been gone for two months Roger and now you show up," she waved her hand about.

"Look, I stayed away because I knew that if we made up then you would have had an issue with me going on a trip with my friends."

"So what was this?" Sasha asked hurt.

"I missed you, this…" he met her gaze, "this wasn't planned okay?'

"No it's not okay, is this all I am to you? A quick lay and then you go run off to your friends again?" Sasha asked angrily and stomped off barefoot to the lounge.

Roger followed after her leisurely, "Sasha wait."

"Wait for what?" Sasha spun around her furious glare penetrating his skull.

"I didn't come here to fight with you," he raised his hands in defence.

"Oh ja, what did you come here for?" Turning around and entered the lounge with him close on her heel.

"I don't even know why I bothered," Roger said deflated. "I think I'll just leave, I don't want to fight."

"Seriously," she asked shocked, "Just leave, run away."

"Bye, Sasha," he said and walked out of the door.

Tears ran down Sasha's face as she silently watched him walk away. The shock of the exchange had immobilised her to the spot.

17

Sasha opened her eyes; everything was blurry. She frantically looked around and spotted the generic floral curtains and powder pink walls; it was supposed to create a comfortable calming atmosphere but it was clearly in contrast to the bright florescent lights that beamed down on her.
"Hi there," the doctor clad in his white lab coat smiled down at her.

"Hello," she replied groggily still a little confused, rubbing her eyes with her right hand before pinching the bridge of my nose in concentration.

"Sash?" Her eyes shot open and followed the sound of her name to the foot of the bed where he is standing and as soon as their eyes met, everything came flooding back.

"It's over," Roger said, forming the words slowly, while tears unwarranted spilled from her eyes.

She shook her head and looked back to the doctor, who was still standing next to her probing and checking her vitals.

"Yes dear, it's over. Everything went well. You will be discharged shortly," he said turning and left the room.

Roger walked over to the side of the bed, taking the doctor's place, he lifted Sasha's hand in his, "it was quick," and as the realization of what she had just done sank in, the finality of the situation bore down on my soul and she sobbed.

"Roger, please call me when you get this message," Sasha said as soon as the message tone beeped.

Again Roger rejected her calls. Sasha felt chills vibrate through her body as she stared at the positive pregnancy test in her hands. She was scared, unsure of what she had to do. She had no one to talk to and the sex-talk her mother gave her 'as jy jags is dan beter jy sien dat jy clinic toe gaan', rang in her ears.

Sasha visited a chemist the following day during her lunch break.

"Can I please have the morning-after pill?" She asked nervously.

"You have to take the tablet immediately," the old pharmacist said sternly.

"Yes, thank you." She thanked the pharmacist and stuffed the little brown bag with the tablet into her bag and headed back to work, visiting the ladies room as soon as she entered the building.

She woke up the following day, her stomach cramping and a little blood on her panties. She assumed the tablet had worked. But when by the month she started vomiting bile every time she brushed her teeth and the smell of the food in the cafeteria made her stomach tighten and had her running to the lavatory to hurl, she knew the tablet had not worked.

The following Friday, Sasha went to Roger's mother's house. Roger was just leaving the house, "Roger?"

He seemed to startle, "Sasha, what are you doing here?"

"You haven't been returning any of my calls or texts," she answered softly casting a look to the house.

He grabbed her by the arm and pulled her toward the car, "let me take you home."

"Stop it, you're hurting me," she whined.

"I'm barely touching you," he glared at her.

Sasha obediently got into the car and waited for him to get into the driver's side.

"What do you want?" He asked through clenched jaws.

"I'm pregnant," she spat out the words, scared that she might not have the courage to say it.

Shock washed over him, he sat staring at her with wide eyes, "What? Is it mine?"

"How dare you? What do you mean is it yours? Who else's would it be?"

He closed his eyes and laid his head on the steering wheel. Sasha sat silently rubbing her hands together on her lap.

"You're getting an abortion!" He declared looking Sasha dead in the eyes.

Now it was Sasha's turn to be shocked.

"I'll take you to the doctor now," he said and started the car.

Once again she felt like a zombie just coasting along.

"There it is, you are definitely pregnant," the doctor said pointing to the little screen by the side of the bed. "It's about 6 weeks." He smiled.

"Can you refer us to a doctor to have the pregnancy terminated please?" Roger asked all business. Sasha was still staring at the screen, gob-smacked, unable to respond or even form words. Her eyes trained on the bean on the screen that was very much a part of her.

"Yes, of course," the doctor turned to Sasha and asked, "if you are sure?"

Sasha looked to Roger, his fierce scowl telling her not to mess with him, she looked back to the doctor and nodded unable to speak.

She shook her head to clear her thoughts and pulled her hand away from Roger.

"Are you okay?" he asked.

"No," she answered abruptly and turned her gaze back to the floral curtains.

"Come on Sasha, it's not that bad."

She turned her angry gaze back to him, "easy for you to say, you are not the one in this bed. You are not the one who just killed," she said and stopped as the wind got caught in her throat, tears running down her cheeks once more. She closed her eyes tightly, trying to stop the tears.

"Baby," Roger said softly and rubbed his hand over her hair.

"Don't call me that," she whispered.

"You are overreacting."

She did not respond she simply just lied there and cried softly. Roger took a seat in the grey fold-up chair next to the bed and scrolled through his phone; until the doctor entered the room about half an hour later.

"Miss. Peters?"

Sasha opened her eyes, "yes doctor."

"I have signed your discharge papers; you may leave whenever you're ready."

"Oh, okay," Sasha said confused, she thought it would take longer for her to be discharged. She needed time to come to terms with what she just did.

Roger got up and shook the doctor's hand.

"You are fine to leave, there's no need to wait."

"Oh, okay. Thank you," she said again softly as the nurse carefully removed the drip from Sasha's hand.

Sasha got out of the bed turning to Roger, "you can wait outside."

"What? Why?" He asked confused.

She steeled him with a fierce scowl. He shook his head and left the room, closing the door behind him.

Sasha and Roger silently walked side by side out of the building.

"I'm sorry, Sasha."

"Yeah, about what?"

"Please I never wanted this to happen."

"You didn't even think about it. You decided to kill our baby, you decided and I let you."

"It wasn't even a baby yet."

"Whatever helps you sleep at night," Sasha said sarcastically and felt her legs tremble.

"That's unfair; we aren't ready to be parents, both of us. It's not just me."

"I guess you got what you wanted, you don't ever have to hear from me again," she said and shakily stumbled, tripping over her feet. Roger caught her before she could fall, "I'm fi.."

Roger caught her limp body as her knees buckled and carried her to his car; she wanted to object but she felt too weak, she silently allowed him to carry her, resting her head on his chest.

"You can let me go now," she insisted when they reached his car.

"You fainted; maybe we should go back inside?" he asked concerned.

"I'm fine; I think it's the blood loss. The doctor said I would feel weak, and just so by the way I did not faint. I feel weak, thank you very much, I feel better now," she explained, pushing past Roger.

"Come on Sasha, sit down for a minute, the blood."

"I'm touched by your concern," she rolled her eyes at him and looked down, "but I am fine, no thanks to you." and stomped off in search of her mother's car.

Roger stood watching her walk away but made no attempt to stop her. He could see her stumble a few steps and wanted to rush to her side to help but let her be. He watched as she got into the car; placed her head on the steering, and cry. It broke his heart that she was in so much pain but he had made his choice and he truly believed that this was the best for both of them. He stood next to his car and watched her, hoping she would look his way. She never did, lifting her head slowly, she wiped the tears from her eyes and cheeks and looked around the cockpit of the car until she pulled a tissue to her nose and blew it before driving away.

18

"Where have you been? I've been calling you all morning." Sasha's mother asked as soon as she walked through the door.

"Sorry, I took so long. I had more work than I thought," Sasha lied feebly, "I'm going to lie down, I am exhausted."

"From gallivanting all morning?"

"I wasn't gallivanting I had to work. Thank you for lending me your car, I'm sorry I took so long." She apologised again, walked to her bedroom running her hand against the wall for balance, the feel of the cold bumpy wall felt good on her fingertips. She closed the door and once inside the solitude of her room, lied on the bed. She felt empty, alone, hurt; surrounded by the dark. The dark of her own decisions, choices, vulnerability and insecurities were her only companions. She thought of Roger and his rapid decision to terminate, of how she blindly went along with it, chastising herself for not being stronger.

She hated Roger for teaching her to love. For awaking feelings and emotions she never knew existed before him. She felt the pain where the drip was inserted sting her hand, a blaring reminder of her failure. Strangely enough that pain made her feel a little better, she thought of how she actually deserved that pain.

She lied there on her bed, looking at the ceiling, refusing to think. Stuffing it all down, way down until there was nothing left. For the first time since waking up that morning, she felt nothing; absolutely nothing.

Thirsty from all the crying she got up a little disorientated and watched as blood spread down her legs. The last remnants of broken soul pooling on the floor.

19

For the next month Sasha trudged around, her legs felt like lead; putting herself together with sticky-tack and glue, or at least that was what it felt like; living on the precipice.

Sasha took casual strolls down the street to the corner tuck-shop, even started shaving her legs again, wearing denim shorts, t-shirt and flip-flops. Her days were spent reading, lying in the sun on the grass, working and recently her favourite activity – eating Chappies, reading the 'did you know' on the little yellow papers. She watched the kids playing in the dirt, even joined in a few times skipping, those small moments creating a glimmer of light in her otherwise dark existence.

Not even the sight of Stacy sitting in the passenger seat of Roger's car one afternoon evoked any emotion. She laughed out loud realising that she just might be dead inside and there he was driving around like nothing happened.

She kept the smile firmly plastered on her face, continued to go to work and even to her own surprise started dating. She was not interested in a relationship; she did not even think that she believed that love existed outside the pages of a book of a perfectly crafted rom-com. It was all lies manufactured to make you crave after something that would inevitable break your spirit. She knew exactly what love was, it was a lie.

But wanting to feel something, anything; she went out on dates. She was so desensitized that even having sex became just something, like any other activity, watching television or reading. There was absolutely nothing special about it.

"Hey Sasha," she was startled, jumping out of the way, walking down the street back home from the tuck-shop with a packet full of Chappies.

She spun around, "Roger? What do you want?"

"I saw you walking, how are you?" He asked casually and Sasha realised that even seeing him in his soccer shorts had no affect on her. His smile which once turned her to putty, were just lips and his dark eyes were just that, eyes.

"I'm fine," she answered turned around and continued walking.

"Wait up, can I walk with you?"

"It's a free country; do whatever you want."

He smiled sheepishly, "you look great, Sash."

"What's that suppose to mean?" She asked without making eye contact with him.

"I miss you," he stuttered a little, "who was that guy that dropped you off at home the other night?" he started asking.

She stopped, turned on him, "oh cut the crap, is Stacy busy? You think I'm going to give you a quick piece? You know what, I don't even care. I've spent way too much time worried about you and you know what it's none of your business"

"Sasha, you were never a quick lay to me. I loved you." He met her angry scowl before continuing, "I just assumed you would always be there, you know, I could do my stuff, I'm... we are young. I thought you would be waiting for me. Is he your boyfriend?"

Sasha's mouth fell open, "why do you care Roger, you left me, so just go fuck yourself and leave me the hell alone. I have nothing more to give you. You've sucked the life right out of me and then you come and tell me this nonsense. Wat is ek 'n vis op jou vistok wat jy net aan 'n lyntjie kan hou? I've had to put my life together and I am barely breathing again and now, now what? What do you want?" She waved her hands around exasperatedly and steeled him with a furious gaze when he laughed.

He pretended to cough concealing the laugh, "I don't want anything, Sash," he said sadly, "I didn't like seeing you with someone else. I know I have no right, but..."

"No you don't." She held up her hand and continued, "Now do me a favour and leave me alone." She said it fervently and walked away, leaving him standing on the side of the road.

She wondered what it was that kept Roger coming back. Did he really think so little of her? Was she so stupid to be sitting and waiting for the breadcrumbs he deemed her worthy of? Or was this, him, all of it just another facet of the cosmic joke on her life?

She could hardly recognise herself, what more was there for him to break or steal? Wasn't it enough that she was allowing these random guys to slowly chip away piece by piece of her body, not even recognising the emptiness in her eyes?

Sasha looked over her body in the mirror, and only saw the husk of what once was and realised that the sad truth was that this was exactly what she deserved.

20

"Sasha, Sasha?" She heard someone call, while she was walking down the street, looking at all the produce sold by the street vendors. She stopped mid stride and scanned the vicinity. She spotted Micky across the road waving at her, smiled, waved and crossed the road. The pebbles on the road made it impossible for her to walk faster than a crawl in her stiletto heels and pencil skirt. The wind blew over her skin, fanning her hair over her face. She brushed it aside and when she looked up she stared into cognac eyes.

"Sasha," Micky greeted.

Sasha reluctantly diverted her gaze to Micky, "hey Micky. Where are you off to?"

"Oh, I'm just wandering around, no place in particular," she smiled shyly, "and you?"

"I met my friend for lunch, hey sorry for my rudeness. This is my friend Chad, Chad Sasha," Micky gestured to the man still standing silently watching them.

Chad extended a hand to Sasha, "good to meet you Sasha." His eyes crinkled at the corners as he smiled.

"Hello, yes pleasure meeting you." Sasha said nervously brushing her hair back from her face, self-consciously.

"Uhm, I'll see you in the office," she said to Micky and made a hasty retreat.

"Sure, see you." Micky said.

"Bye Sasha," Chad said his gaze running over her body and resting on her eyes, searching.

Sasha felt heat flood her cheeks and quickly looked away, rushing off and headed back to the office.

Her hands were shaking; she wondered what was wrong with her. She did not know Chad from a bar of soap and yet, there she was thinking of him. She wondered whether it was attraction, no it could not be. He was way too short, taller than her but still shorter than what she was used to go for. The way his black turtle-neck top hugged his figure and the way his pants hung from his hips was simply yummy. She laughed a little thinking how ridiculous she was being, she would probably never see him again. His eyes though, there was something about the way he looked at her, it unsettled her and made her feel exposed like he could see right down in the depths of all she hid. It did not matter in any case.

She was still mulling over it when Micky walked in and plopped himself on his chair.

"Have fun?" She asked.

"Yeah," he answered and smiled, "Chad said bye," and winked.

She rolled her eyes, "oh grow up Micky."

"What, I was just passing on the message," he shrugged. "By the way, I gave him your number."

"You what?" Sasha asked a little louder than she expected, quickly looking around the room and fixed Micky with a stare, "why?"

"He asked for it."

"But why?"

"Geez Sasha, I don't know, maybe he likes you, maybe he wants a bread recipe. Ask him when he calls you."

Sasha giggled a little, "bread recipe?"

"Yes, bread or vetkoek." He joined in laughter.

"You are so silly," she laughed.

"In all seriousness, I think he likes you."

"He doesn't know me," she retorted softly.

He slapped his forehead exasperated, "hence the phone number exchange."

"So how do you guys know each other?" She asked curiously.

"We worked together before I started here. He still works there, but our friendship has lasted."

"Oh."

Micky looked over at her, "you know what I don't understand?"

"What?"

"How can a girl or rather woman like you be so completely unaware of how pretty she is?"

Sasha shrugged disbelievingly.

"You are pretty; you have to know how the guys react when you are around?"

"Don't really care, I'm not interested."

"Really? All girls are interested in happily-ever-after."

"There's no such thing as happily-ever-after."

Micky was stunned but made no comment.

21

S asha danced around the kitchen in her pyjamas on Saturday morning, music blaring over the speakers, heating pizza from the previous evening's dinner in the microwave. Her hair was in a messy bun as she floated across the room in bunny slippers. She hardly heard her phone ring, only seeing the flashing light.

"Hello," she yelled into the phone, quickly running to the lounge to turn down the music. "Sorry, hold one second please." She slipped on the tiles and almost landed on her butt, catching herself on the coffee table.

"Hello, sorry, are you still there?" she asked breathlessly.

"Hi, Sasha?"

"Yes, this is she." She rolled her eyes thinking how she almost fell on her ass for another holiday or mobile promotion, annoying call.

"It's Chad," he hesitated for a second, "Micky's friend. I met you the other day."

"Oh, yes. Hi Chad, how can I help you?"

"Geez you don't have to sound so formal," he laughed a little as he teased.

"uhm, sorry. What am I suppose to say?" She asked as she slowly walked back to the kitchen, stopped the microwave and returned to the lounge where she plopped herself onto the sofa.

"No it's fine, I was just teasing. How are you?"

"I'm well thanks and you?"

"I'm good," he answered then were both quiet.

"Uhm, was there a specific reason you called?" Sasha asked feeling awkward.

"No, not really. I just wanted to say hi."

"Why?"

"Just, do you mind?"

"No, uh sorry was that rude?"

"It's fine, guess if I were you, I would be rude too."

She laughed before stating, "You are terrible, you should have said that I wasn't rude."

He joined the laugher, "yeah, maybe not the most gentlemanly response was it."

"Gentlemanly, really? Do gentlemen still exist?"

"Yes, who have you been around?"

His question was meant as rhetoric but she answered anyway, "You have no idea," mulling the question over in her mind. "Do I look like a rude person?" she countered.

"No," he kept quiet but the silence was loaded.

"But? I can hear the but hanging in the air. There's always somebody's big but in the way."

"No buts, it's just." He stopped again.

"What? Just say what you want to say," Sasha felt annoyed.

"Okay, klim van jou perdjie af, you looked sad."

"Sad?" She ran over the entire meeting in her mind and clearly remembered smiling.

"Maybe not sad, more like lonely. You know what I mean?"

"I don't know what you mean."

"Oh I think you know what I mean, but I won't push it."

"I think I have to go," she was uncomfortable and was looking for an escape.

"Don't run away, I have a feeling you've been hiding and running for a long time."

"You don't know me, you met me for what? Two minutes."

"It doesn't matter, I recognised a kindred spirit."

Sasha had no idea how to respond, she sat dumbstruck nervously chewing on her cuticle skin.

"Sasha, you still there? Hello?"

"Yes, I'm here," she answered angrily; she wondered who this guy thought he was that acted as if he knew her.

He laughed quietly, "I'm sorry for offending you. It was not my intention."

"No I'm sorry; I don't know why I got upset."

"I have a theory, you want to hear?"

"Sure, why not?"

"I think you got upset because I touched a nerve."

"I am not that sensitive," Sasha interjected.

"Will you let me finish? You are rude, you know?" Chad teased.

"Fine, I'm rude, carry on," she smiled.

"I think that you've been hurt and now you hide behind a lonely smile, a beautiful one at that don't get me wrong but, lonely. I saw the emptiness in your eyes."

Sasha swallowed hard, "I see." She fumbled over her words, "where are you from Chad?" She sounded sad to her own ears and cleared her throat.

"I'm from Johannesburg," he answered sincerely.

"Aren't we all?" she asked sarcastically.

"No, I believe it's referred to as Gauteng now," he joked easily.

"Very funny," she giggled, "where in Johannesburg exactly are you from?"

"Ah, clear and concise."

"Bugger off," Sasha waved her hand in the air. "You are acting like it's a state secret," she complained.

"State no, maybe national," he laughed loudly, "I live in Roodepoort."

"Roodepoort? That's far."

"Far from?"

"Everything," she mused lying upside down on the couch, her legs resting on the backrest.

"Not necessarily, where do you live?"

"Aan die gatkant van Gauteng, in Brakpan."

"Well if you put it that way, then yes, it is far," he conceded and laughed.

"I really have to go now and no I am not running away. Thanks for the call Chad."

"Would you mind if I called again?"

"Not at all," she said and meant it. "Chat soon."

"Ciao."

22

Chats with Chad became common place. They exchanged calls on a daily basis. It amazed Sasha that she was so comfortable talking with someone she had only met briefly. It became the highlight of her day.

"Hey how was your day?" Sasha asked as soon as she answered the phone, walking out of the house to sit on the wall outside for privacy.

"You sound chirpy; my day was long and yours?" Chad asked casually laying on his bed.

"Same old same old, hey you know what?" Sasha asked excitedly.

"What?" he smiled at her obvious excitement.

"I'm going to buy a car. I've been saving for what seems like forever but I finally have enough for a deposit. Any suggestions?"

"That's great. I can't suggest anything; you have to choose what you like. I can't unduly influence you."

"Please, as if you could influence me," she joked swinging her legs.

"Is that a dare?" Chad asked darkly.

She swallowed hard, "uh, no."

He laughed again, "Scared?"

"No," she answered quickly and then laughed at the sudden flutter of nerves at the pit of her stomach.

"So what are you planning on getting?"

"Getting?" she was so distracted by the unexpected nerves.

"Car, remember?"

"Oh duh," she giggled a little, "I was looking at a Polo this afternoon. What you think about that?"

"Polos are great cars, what did your dad say?"

"I didn't ask him," She hesitated and shrugged, "maybe I'll ask. I'm going to the car dealership on Saturday, I'm so excited."

"I can imagine."

They were both quiet for a while both resigned to their thoughts.

Chad broke the silence, "I want to see you."

"Really?"

"Why does that surprise you?"

"I don't know."

"Let me guess, you are wondering why?"

"You are very intuitive, aren't you?" Sasha asked sarcastically.

"I am an intelligent man, among other things."

"Aren't you confident…?"

"Confidence is sexy."

"I don't even think I reside on the same planet as confidence," she replied jokingly.

"Why do you do that? Why do you think so little of yourself?" he asked concerned.

"I don't, I've just learnt from past experience," she answered nonchalantly. Not looking for sympathy just accepting her reality.

"We've all had our fair share of disappointments and heartaches but, don't let that cloud the way you look at the future or even the way you see yourself."

"I've just accepted my fate. I was never meant for fairytales and happy endings."

"You were meant for anything you want," Chad retorted sitting up on his bed.

"I beg to differ. You can want something with all your heart, does not mean you'll get it. Like for example, you can want to win the lotto but that does not mean that you'll win it."

"Yes, but I can counter, that you might win the lotto, if you actually buy a ticket. You can't win if you don't play."

"So you're saying that I've given up without trying?" Sasha asked rubbing her shoulders, casting a glance over at the bugs crowding around the light.

"I don't pretend to know what you've been through but, I have to believe that despite the disappointments, that there is still some semblance of hope in there somewhere."

"I wish I could say that there was, but I don't feel anything anymore. I am empty; I have no more to give." She admitted sadly before getting off the wall, entering the house and headed straight to her bedroom.

Chad sighed softly, "I'm not expecting you to give anything, on the contrary," he paused lying back down on the bed, "I want to give you so much."

Sasha laughed sadly, "Why me? You don't even know me?"

"I saw the magic in your eyes."

"I don't get it."

"Can I see you? Lunch maybe?" Chad asked hopeful.

Sasha felt self conscious and suddenly scared to see him. She had not even thought of Chad in that way. She

assumed he enjoyed chatting with her, how the
conversation had taken such a sharp turn, she was unsure,
a turn in a direction that Sasha was too afraid of going.
She knew where it would lead, hurt, pain, regret, and
inevitably loss.

"Come on, just lunch?" Chad asked softly again,
sensing her internal struggle.

"I don't know, you don't know me."

"That's just an excuse, I know you well enough.
You're intelligent, your fast wit, funny, and I sense that
you have an open mind and that is hard to find."

"Oh," she did not know how to respond to that.

"Say yes. Stop your mind from going to no, instead just
say yes."

"Okay," Sasha agreed reluctantly, "lunch".

"Cool, I'll see you tomorrow."

"Tomorrow?"

"Yes, I'm not giving you a chance to change your
mind. I'll be waiting outside your building at 12?"

Sasha laughed softly, "sure, sure. See you tomorrow."

23

S asha stood in the foyer looking out through the glass doors of the office, clutching her stomach. She could see Chad casually leaning against the balustrade waiting for her. She took a deep breath and straightened her black cocktail-dress before taking a step forward. As she emerged from the building into the blinding sun, the heel of her red stiletto caught between the tiles on the stairs and she plunged head first forward. Throwing her hands forward, when her knees collided against the concrete floor.

"Eina," she complained on all fours.

"Sasha," Chad extended a hand to help her up.

She pinched her eyes shut in embarrassment, "Oh goodness, tell me you didn't see that?"

"Are you okay?"

Wiping her hands on her dress, "I'm fine."

He did not question her any further, instead patiently waited for her to collect herself. She looked at him shyly, "sorry, I'm ready to go."

"Since we only have an hour, I figured we'll go to that Italian bistro two blocks away."

"I love that place, the food is delicious," she smiled happily.

"Great, shall we?"

"Sure."

They walked quietly side by side, each stealing sideways glances intermittently.

"You are way more talkative on the phone," Chad noted as the waiter showed them to their table in the far corner in the back of the restaurant.

"Maybe it's because I'm hungry," she stuck her tongue out at him.

He laughed a little, exposing the tip of his tongue between his teeth, "then we should feed you." He tapped the menu, "order quickly."

"Oh please, scared I might bite you?"

"I wish you would," he said and winked, enjoying the shocked look on Sasha's face.

She swallowed hard and quickly hid behind the menu. Chad laughed quietly as Sasha felt heat flood her cheeks. Clearing her throat, she peeked over the menu, "you know you are very forward."

He feigned innocence, "me?"

The rest of lunch went by swimmingly, they chatted and before they knew it, it was time to head back to the office.

"That was lovely, thank you." Sasha thanked.

"It really was thank you for joining me."

"As if I had a choice," she rolled her eyes jokingly.

"You always have a choice," he said sombrely.

"I was just joking."

"I know."

"I'm sorry; I didn't mean to spoil…" she started to say when Chad interjected, "you don't have to apologise. Why do you always do that?"

"Do what? Put my foot in my mouth?"

"No, why do you so easily accept blame?" He asked as they stopped at the corner, waiting for the traffic light to change colour.

Sasha looked up at the light and shrugged. Chad shook his head and they walked on quietly, both resigned to their thoughts.

When they approached her office, she looked up sadly at Chad, "thank you for lunch, Chad. I really enjoyed it."

He looked at her for a second, searching her eyes. He took her hand in his and lifted it, watching her focus follow the ascent of her hand, their hands intertwined in front of them, "thank you, Sasha."

She blushed slightly, "pleasure," and diverted her gaze to the glass doors of the building, "I have to go now."

"Call you later?"

"Sure, laters," she answered smiling shyly.

He pulled her closer to him and placed his left hand gently on her cheek, leaned in and kissed her softly on the lips. She closed her eyes as their lips touched; he took a step back and smiled as she opened her eyes slowly.

"Bye Sasha," he smiled, turned and walked away.

Sasha touched her lips watching his retreating back and as he ran across the road she turned, headed up the two stairs and into the building.

She slowly climbed the stairs to their office. She felt confused. Why had he kissed her? Why did it even bother her? She enjoyed his company, particularly their conversations. As she placed her foot on the landing on her office's floor, she froze mid-stride. Her breath caught in her throat as realisation dawned on her. She coughed as she choked on the air, she held onto the railing for balance.

"Shit!" she exclaimed softly and shook her head, to clear her thoughts but also in rejection of those same thoughts.

She wanted him to kiss her; she had felt so connected to him, like she could see right down to her own soul as she looked into his eyes, a kindred spirit. There was something about him that called to her and this realisation scared her shitless.

24

Panic washed over Sasha every time her phone rang. She would slowly lift it to check the caller id and would quickly press ignore or simply let it go to her voicemail, whenever Chad's name flickered across the screen.

Guiltily listening to the messages:

"Hey Sasha, it's Chad. Please call me, when you get this message."

"Hi, me again. Just wanted to know whether you're okay?"

"Okay, seriously I am getting worried. Are you okay?"

"Dammit Sasha, are you mad at me? Did I do something wrong?"

"Is it the kiss?"

With each new message, Sasha felt more and more guilty. She did not know how to respond, she did not know what to say.

I know that you've heard my messages.

Sasha, please?

After two weeks of ignoring Chad, Sasha finally built up enough courage to respond, she was not brave enough to talk to him yet instead, she typed slowly, her hands shaking.

Hi Chad, I am sorry for the silence. I needed time to think. I don't think I can see you again. It has nothing to do with you, it's me. I'm sorry. Good bye.

By the time she pressed the send button, a lone tear slowly and silently slid down her cheek. She sat staring at the screen but there was no response. She knew in her heart of hearts it was the right thing to do, but it hurt like hell and that pain only confirmed it, if she allowed herself to feel any more for Chad than she already did, it would inevitably end in an unspeakable pain, that she knew she would not be able to handle.

The next morning she woke to the message light flickering on her phone, her heart skipped a beat as she opened her messenger.

3 Unread messages:

You're using a break-up line on me lol.

Next message:

You're serious ;-(

Next:

I understand Sasha, you're scared. I sensed it the first time I met you. I could see it in your eyes. I cannot begin to imagine what has caused it but I will never push or pressurise you. I am happy to just chat, if that's okay? Take the time you need, I'll be here. I will wait, you are worth the wait. Chad

She read and reread his responses a few times before responding,

Sasha: *I don't understand you...*

Chad: *Ask me anything you like, see if I can clarify.*

Sasha: *Why me?*

Chad: *Why not? You are a remarkable person.*

Sasha: *There's nothing remarkable about me.*

Chad: *That's the point you are to me... Everything about you draws me in, it's like magic.*

Sasha: *That's just not true.*

She sat up in bed, hugging her duvet tight to her chest as tears streamed over her cheeks.

Chad: *Your magic enthrals...*

Sasha: *See, this is what I struggle with. Why me? Why are you wasting your time with me? I am no good. You are such a great guy, you deserve so much better than me.*

Chad: *Maybe I'm no good as well or maybe you're just putting me on a pedestal, when all I am is a regular Joe with warts just like everybody else. Why do you think you are no good?*

Sasha: *You don't want to jump into this dark abyss, believe me. I don't want to poison you.*

Chad: *You can do whatever you like with me... lol There is darkness in all of us, Sasha. We just have to learn to find the beauty in that darkness.*

Sasha: *I have to go.* She sent the last message with no promises, switched off her phone and laid her head back against her headboard.

25

There is beauty in darkness, Sasha scribbled on a notepad, lying on the grass in the front yard, chewing on the end of her yellow Bic pen. *What does that even mean?* She wondered, dejectedly getting up off the floor. The grass left imprints on her thighs, she sighed looking at it, annoyed by her inability to figure out the conundrum. Stalking off to her car parked in the driveway facing the street, she got into the driver's side and stuffed her notebook into the crevice on the side of the door panel and stuck the pen into the messy bun on her head, a few tendrils sticking out around the sides. Sasha reclined her seat, turned on the music, lied back and closed her eyes.

"Sasha?"

She was startled by the sound of her name, her eyes shot open. She had not even realised that she had fallen asleep, "mmh?" She asked looking around the car, her gaze landing on the person standing next to the open window. "Chad?" she looked around frantically, "what, uhm, what are you doing here?" She wiped her eyes.

He smiled cockily, "sorry to disturb your nap. You were snoring so loud, I had to come check what the commotion was about," and laughed a little.

Sasha felt heat flood her cheeks and smiled, "sorry," and wiped the dribble of drool from the side of her mouth, "I don't snore."

"Then why say sorry?" He teased raising an eyebrow.

"Uhm. What are you doing here?" She asked again.

"I was in the neighbourhood," he shrugged.

Rolling her eyes, "ja right, nogal in the neighbourhood. Seriously though, what are you doing here?"

"I wanted to see where you live, you always speak so fondly of the area," he raised his hands defensively, "okay, okay, I drove pass your house and I recognized your car, I figured I check if it was yours and low-and-behold there you were sitting in the car. I swear I wouldn't have stopped if I didn't see you. But, real talk, I was just curious and decided to take a drive."

"Oh." Sasha looked over her bare legs and tank top.

"You look beautiful," he announced tucking a loose tendril of hair behind her ear through the open window, as he noticed her disapproving once-over.

His touch was electrifying, turning her cheeks beet red. She reached for the door handle, "Uhm, let me get out. Excuse me?"

Chad took a step back and watched as she opened the door and got out of the car. The little notebook fell out of the crevice and before Sasha could stoop to pick it up, Chad snatched it off the ground, "there is beauty in darkness," he read aloud raising an eyebrow questioningly.

"It's what you said the other day," she shrugged, "I can't figure out what you meant and it's bothering me."

"I see," he said and followed her to the boundary wall, where he casually leaned over the wall, resting on his elbows. "What about it is bothering you?"

"What do you mean with darkness?" She asked hopping onto the wall facing Chad, swinging her legs looking at him intently.

"Darkness can mean a lot of things. People generally associate the dark with bad," he shook his head, "I believe that to be a very narrow way of looking at it," he started explaining and stopped, casting a glance at Sasha, who was still silently listening to him. "We go through life making choices, experience after experience, decisions that change the course or directions of our lives. Bad and good, but whenever we experience anything bad, we tend to do one of two things, we learn from it or we try to avoid it altogether."

"But isn't that just instinctive though? It's normal to want to avoid something that hurt you." Sasha countered.

"Yes and no," Chad smiled revealing the tip of his tongue ever so slightly.

She returned a smile, her gaze fixed on the pink of his tongue, "go ahead, explain yourself." She waved her hand to exaggerate the statement.

Chad laughed softly, "You're cute when you're bossy," He laughed loudly at her reaction and held up his hand in defence, "okay, okay. What was I saying again?"

Sasha rolled her eyes, "Yes, no, darkness?"

"Oh ja, okay. Yes, it's instinct to protect yourself. It's good even but leads to the reason why I say no, because we take it too far. We remove ourselves from everything, we cease to live we just merely exist."

"Existing isn't so bad," Sasha conceded sadly, her smile mangling on her face.

"No, it's not," he shrugged, "for a while at least." He searched her eyes and for a moment it seemed as if time stood still. Sasha's face was flushed before she averted her gaze, looking at the grass.

He followed her gaze, both resigned to their thoughts. "You have such cute toes," he muttered appreciatively.

She tried hiding her feet and almost fell off the wall. Chad wrapped his right arm around her waist and caught her, "watch out," he said with laughter in his voice.

"Thanks, don't look at my feet."

"Why? It's cute."

She blushed crimson, "noooo! What is it about guys and toes? Jissie."

Chad laughed as Sasha struggled to hide her feet still restricted by his arm around her waist. He gently lifted her off the wall and swung her around, while they laughed. Before putting her down, her hands still wrapped around his neck, bodies flush. He wasn't very tall but she still had to tilt her head up to look into his eyes, he met her gaze and placed a soft swift kiss on her lips.

"Chad," she whispered softly taking a step back.

"I'm sorry," he started saying and stopped short, "no, I lie, I'm not sorry." He touched her cheek.

"No, I'm sorry Chad," she looked away, "I am not worth your affection."

"Why do you think that?" He asked.

"Do you want to come inside?" Sasha gestured to the door.

"Sure."

"Make yourself at home, can I get you anything?"

"No thanks Sash," he took a seat on the sofa and watched as she plopped herself on the armchair. "Why do you think you aren't worth it?"

She shrugged, "past experiences."

"The past should stay in the past."

She nodded.

"Enlighten me Sasha, what past experience makes you believe that you are not worthy?"

"I can't," she said looking at her hands on her lap. She looked up and met Chad's gaze. For a second he was lost in the pain swimming in her eyes. He got up and walked over to the arm chair, sat down on the armrest.

"You don't have to say anything," he swiped a tendril of her hair behind her ear and continued, "nothing you have done or that was done to you, defines who you are and it definitely does not determine your worth."

"Thanks," she said as a tear silently slid over her cheek. Sasha rested her face in her hands, hiding from Chad's prying eyes. "I, I had an abortion," the words poured out of her as she confessed to her deepest darkest secret.

Chad stroked her hair, "do you want to talk about it?"

She looked up at him, sorrow her predominant feature, "It was my entire fault."

"You always take the blame for everything, don't you?"

She shrugged, "It is what it is."

"Why do you say it's your fault?"

"Because it is."

"Okay then, tell me what happened?"

She looked at him quizzically, "does it matter, I know what you think of me now."

"Firstly, how could you? Can you read my mind?" he smiled sheepishly. "Secondly, talking about it might help you move past it, but you don't have to if you don't want to."

Sasha smiled sadly, "It's a long story."

"I have time," he looked at his watch, "or do you want me to leave?"

"No! You don't have to go. Okay, let's see, where does one begin?"

Chad got up and took a seat on the sofa across from her once more, "I want to see you."

"Oh, okay. I fell pregnant after my ex broke up with me and then he said that I should have an abortion and I just agreed because I was scared,"

"mmmh, your ex broke up with you because you got pregnant?"

"No, he broke up with me before that happened. I don't think I'm explaining it right. Okay forget the break up, I got pregnant and he freaked out and demanded that I have an abortion and I just went along with it."

"So what exactly is your fault, in this scenario?"

"The," she waved her hand about, "everything."

"You were scared, what else were you going to do? And for the record, I don't think less of you, if anything I think so much more of you. Your ex is an ass and he forced you."

"No he didn't force me," she interrupted and shook her head.

"He didn't exactly give you a choice either. Any man worth that title would have supported you and given you the choice. It isn't your fault that he wasn't man enough to step up."

Sasha sat stoned face looking at Chad.

Chad smiled reassuringly before continuing, "Your mistakes or failures do not define you, how you rise and move on from there does. Don't let your past keep you hostage Sasha. Grieve, cry, and scream you made a mistake, but eventually you have to move on from it."

26

"What a nice boy that was yesterday, Chuck?" Sasha's mother commented.

"Chad, yes, he's a great guy."

"Oh Chad, are you dating?"

"No, he's a friend," Sasha answered nonchalantly while drying the dishes.

Her mother rolled her eyes, "oh. Do you like him?"

Sasha's mouth fell open as she stared at her mother.

"What? Can't I ask?" Her mother laughed at her expression.

"Oh you can ask, I just don't know whether I can answer."

"Well, see that right there is answer enough," her mom winked at her.

"Ma, can I ask you something?"

"You already are?"

"Something else?"

"Sure."

"Was daddy your only boyfriend?"

"No, but I wasn't dating a parade of men either," her mother answered sarcastically. "Chad seems like a nice guy, how old is he?"

"He's 27," Sasha answered softly not knowing what her mother's response would be.

Her mother's mouth dropped open, "he doesn't look that old. But he is five years older than you."

"Yes, but they say age is just a number." Sasha shrugged and hopped onto the counter.

"He is way too old for you," she steeled Sasha with a cold stare.

Sasha looked down sadly, "I don't think so, he understands me."

"He understands you?" her mother scoffed. "Understands what?"

"I can't explain it, he is different. Ma?"

"mmmh?" her mother responded over her shoulder stirring the pot.

"Why haven't we ever spoken like this?"

Her mother turned around wiping her hands on the dish cloth, "we've never had anything to talk about before and you never seem to want to."

Sasha blinked rapidly at her mother's response. *Do I really not want to talk to her? Miskien het ek regtig 'n afswitch gesig.* She thought watching her mother move around the kitchen.

27

As night settled over the rooftops, Sasha watched as one by one street light lit up. She swung her legs back and forth over the wall completely lost in thought. She inhaled deeply, savouring the smell of the coming rain, letting her hair hang down her back, the breeze blowing over her heated skin.

Have I changed? I even had a decent conversation with mom. Wat het oor haar lewer geloop? She giggled softly. Her thoughts turned back to the conversation she had with Chad and his unexpected visit. *What is it with this guy? Why won't he stay away? But then do I even want him to stay away?* She smiled shyly, *he is rather cute, can't believe I wasn't attracted to him from the get-go. Was I so desensitized, talk about being dof. My darkness must have been so all consuming. But maybe Chad is right; I just have to find the beauty in my darkness.* She cringed at the thought and wrapped her arms around her torso rubbing her shoulders as the cold breeze blew over her skin, leaving goosebumps in its wake. It was getting dark rapidly because of the rain clouds but still Sasha sat on the wall oblivious to the rain that threatened mulling over her thoughts.

For a few moments her mind went blank, devoid of thoughts, questions, or anything. She felt free for the first time in what seemed like forever.

Is life really that simple? Can I choose to be happy? Can I choose to just be?

"Aahhh!" She yelled as a giant raindrop plopped right on her forehead. She jumped off the wall and landed on all fours, laughing jubilantly as the raindrops dripped, dripped, dropped all over her body. She did not even care that her clumsiness had her technically fall off the wall. She wiped her hands off on her thighs as she got up from the ground. She looked up at the dark clouds hovering above and ran to the gate, heading back into the yard and house. Once inside she headed to the bathroom to wash her hands and trotted leisurely back to her bedroom.

"Hello?" A sing-song female voice answered Chad's phone.

Sasha looked at the screen of her phone to make sure she dialled the correct number. She swallowed hard, "Uhm, hello." She answered unsure.

"Yes, can I help you?"

"No," Sasha cleared her throat, "I think I dialled the wrong number, sorry." She hung up without waiting for a response. She threw the phone down on her bed stunned. The phone rang almost as soon as it hit the mattress, but Sasha refused to answer. She just stood next to the bed

watching his name flicker across the screen, her throat
thick from unshed tears.

The Dark

28

"I am such an idiot," she whispered through clenched jaws. She wrestled with herself, fought to keep the tears that threatened at bay; instead she chose to be angry. She felt betrayed, she had opened up to him, exposed her secrets, her insecurities, her failures, and now what?

"I'll wait for you, imagine, what a load of crap," she proclaimed before lying on her bed and burying her face in her pillow. "Idiot, idiot, idiot," she proclaimed muffled by the pillow.

The phone rang again and this time she grabbed it off the pedestal and flung it against the wall. She watched as the screen cracked and landed on the laminate floor with a thud. "Shit!" she exclaimed jumping up and running to the phone. "See, a damn fool," she rolled her eyes and tried to unlock the phone but the crack in the touch screen was buggered. It rang again but she was unable to answer.

"Come on," she said exasperated to the universe and burst out laughing.

She sat on the floor laughing until the tears started rolling down her face and thoughts of Chad with another woman taunted her. Sadness enveloped her like a glove, as the tears ebbed while she silently listened to the raindrops falling, the thunder cracked and she watched the lighting whip across the sky and light up her room. She admired the beauty of it all, the sounds, and the smell. She appreciated the changes it made to the day.

She sat silently crossed legged on the floor, looking out through her window, admiring it all.

This really is beautiful. She thought and as the lighting struck once more, she had an epiphany. "Shit!" she exclaimed and quickly placed her hand over her mouth to muffle the sound. She laughed, "geez, I am so dof," she giggled.

She scrambled off the floor and made a beeline to her dressers, found her notebook and pen in the draw. Took a seat by the desk facing the window, smiled and wrote:

I am blind. I have been blind for all my life. I look at my life and think of how I've always just thought of it as being handed to me from some greater or higher power. I've let myself down. Watching the rain fall, the thunder crack and lightening break across the sky, those are all part of nature, science... It all happens for a reason.

I've been through a lot in my very short life, not all always good but as Chad said I take blame very easily. I finally realise that I am not to blame for everything but what I am to blame, is giving things, people, situations, and whatever else the power over my happiness.

I over-think the most simplistic things. I don't fit in anywhere, not even my family but does that make me worthless? Why do I diminish myself to make people feel better? Why am I such a people pleaser?

Sasha looked up from her notebook, still clasping the pen tightly. She swiped her hair back from her face and jumped as thunder roared through her bedroom and with a loud bang tripped the electricity. She was suddenly surrounded by darkness and for the first time, she did not feel suffocated by it. The relief of her light-bulb moment was freeing. She grabbed her phone trying to use the built-in flashlight and laughed when she could not access it because of the gigantic crack running across the screen. Pushing away from the desk, she rushed from her room in search of a candle and stubbed her toe with the door as she opened it, "Eina!" she screamed, jumping around on one foot rubbing her toe.

Her father was standing at the fuse box, "it's out by the main box." He declared over his shoulder, "you okay?" He asked Sasha shining his flashlight on her.

"Ek het my toon gestamp," she said releasing her foot, "ek gaan kerse haal."

"Okay, Hop along," he teased and laughed.

She rolled her eyes and headed for the kitchen, returning with a hand full of candles, she handed a few to her father and headed to her room with one. Sasha lit the candle as soon as she got back inside and placed it on the desk next to her notebook. She sat poised with her pen in hand and watched the light from the flame dance over the page.

I finally get it. There is beauty in the dark. The darkest clouds produce the most rain, rain that brings life, feeds crops, even the clichéd darkest berry is always the sweetest, she laughed quietly, *they say the darkest chocolate is the healthiest,* "blegh," she said sticking out her tongue. *I don't like dark chocolate but it adds to my point.*

My darkness is not the mistakes I've made but the weirdness I feel, the fact that I don't fit in etc. does not define me. I have beauty inside me. I am brave, my darkness makes me brave and the scars I bare are proof that I am strong; it proves that I was stronger than whatever tried to break or ruin me. I might not have made the best decisions but from this day I choose to not hand over my happiness to anybody. I might not have known how to love myself, but starting today I will try.

Sasha sat back in her chair and chewed on the tip of the pen. She felt like a new person, looking at life through new eyes. For the first time her eyes were opened. She thought of how Chad had tried to tell her all these things and felt sad once more when she remembered how she finally got to this revelation… A woman answered his phone. *I have no right to feel hurt, he does not owe me anything,* she thought. *I have pushed him away on so many occasions.* She smiled then, *he did help me see… and for that I will ever be grateful.*

Sasha pushed her chair back almost falling tea-over-kettle and laughed, "Wish my epiphany came with some balance for me." She inhaled deeply and released it slowly.

29

"Hey Micky," Sasha greeted cheerily as she entered the office.

"Well, hey pretty lady. You look beautiful today." Micky turned his questioning gaze to Sasha.

She curtsied, "why thank you kind Sir."

"Somebody got it all this morning, huh?"

"Yes, I ate all my Kellogs. I even drank the milk," she answered and winked.

He laughed, got up and asked, "you want some coffee?"

"Sure, lemme just switch on my pc, I'll be right with you." She locked her bag in the credenza and made her way to the kitchen, where Micky was waiting for the water to boil, "Mick, do you know where I can have my phone repaired?"

"What happened to your phone?"

"I dropped it accidentally," Sasha shrugged, "the screen cracked, now I can't do anything with it. See?"

She handed him the phone and watched as he examined it.

"I know a guy actually."

"How long do you think it'll take?"

"I'm not sure, I'll call him."

They walked back to their respective desks sipping their coffees. "That'll be awesome, I feel incomplete without my phone."

Her office line rang, reception informing her that she had a guest waiting downstairs. Avoiding the ancient elevators, she walked down the stairs slowly, stopping dead in her tracks as she emerged from the stairwell. She composed herself, taking a deep breath and walked over to the reception waiting area.

"Chad," Sasha almost whispered his name and smiled.

"Sasha, hi." He vacated the seat and walked toward her closing the short distance between them.

"Hi," she said clearing her throat, "how are you?"

He raised an eyebrow questioningly, "I'm well thanks, I called you a million times."

"I saw," she started saying when Chad cut her short.

"I need to explain."

She raised her hand silencing him, "no, no, you don't. You don't owe me anything."

"Yeah, but I want to. Listen, last night when you called."

"It's fine, Chad."

"No, will you please just let me explain."

Sasha giggled, "Sorry, can we sit at least?"

Chad looked around, "Oh, yes." The reception was empty so they sat next to each other, huddled closely together. "When you called last night, my sister answered my phone."

Sasha laughed, "Your sister?"

"Yes, my sister. I was in the shower. I got caught in the rain and needed to wash off."

"Oh," Sasha said.

He took her hand in his and looked her deeply in her eyes, "I know what you must have thought and your inclination to run away from me," he smiled sheepishly.

Sasha smiled, "I have to be honest, my mind went to the worst places but I realised that I didn't care," Chad looked at her confused, as she continued, "not like that. I mean, I realised that we've never made anything official," she shrugged, "and I can't expect you to sit around waiting for me."

"But that's exactly what I said I would do, you are worth the wait to me. I wish you could see yourself through my eyes?" He closed his eyes resigned.

"This is what I am trying to tell you," Sasha said waiting for him to look at her.

"I had an epiphany last night," she smiled shyly; "I finally understand what you meant when you said that there is beauty in darkness. I won't go into it all right now. But I want to thank you for helping me find my way and after I called and the woman, your sister answered, I was drowning in my own misery," she laughed silently, "I thought that I had missed my shot with you, because of my own stupidity. But during the course of the night, I was reborn, I emerged from my darkness a new person."

"So why didn't you answer the phone?" He asked.

"That's a little embarrassing," she blushed.

"Now I'm intrigued."

"I was devastated after the call," she closed her eyes, "and I threw my phone against the wall and the screen cracked and I couldn't access anything on it."

Chad was silent. Sasha peeked through the slits of her fingers.

"What?" Sasha asked, seeing the cocky grin on Chad's face.

"You threw you phone against the wall for me?"

"Oh get over yourself," she said dropping her face in her hands.

"I like that you were jealous," he teased.

"I'm only human." She said and saw the time on the wall, "shit, I have to get to back to work."

"Sure, can we hook up tonight? I think we have a few more things to discuss. Do you want to go for dinner or must I come to your house?"

"No," She said thoughtful.

"You don't want to?"

"No man, geez, give me a second, I'm thinking. I don't think this is a conversation for a restaurant and I definitely don't want to talk with my parents in the next room."

Chad interjected, "Oh okay, you want to come over to my place? I promise to be good," and winked.

"That's okay, I can cook for you." Sasha offered.

"Cool, see you tonight."

"Drop me a pin, I'll see you tonight."

They exchanged an enthusiastic smile; Chad leaned forward and gave Sasha a kiss on the cheek.

They got up, hugged and headed on to the rest of their day.

Back in the office, time sped by. When Sasha finally looked at her watch, it was already 4 o'clock. She hadn't even thought of what she could cook for Chad. Shock-stricken, she panicked *how could I have offered to cook, I don't even know what he has in his house.* Sasha sat with her head in her hands. "I should cancel…" she winced and lifted the receiver, waiting for Chad to answer.

"Chad speaking, how may I assist you? Hello?"

"Uhm, hello," Sasha stuttered, fear gripping her throat.

"Sash?"

She cleared her throat, "yes."

"Oh hey, I'm just wrapping up here at work. I completely forgot to send you the pin. But your phone is broken, right? How about I just come around your office and then you can follow me?"

He continued filling the silence, "or do you rather want to leave your car at the office? I can always drive you home after? Sasha?"

"Mmmh, uhm, I was thinking maybe we should do it another day."

"Ahh come on Sash, don't go chicken on me now," he teased and continued, "no pressure Sash, it'll be fun and you can leave whenever you like."

"I'm doing it again, aren't I?"

Chad laughed quietly, "So I'll see you shortly. Bye Sash, let me finish up here."

Sasha was parked on the curb in front of her office building waiting for Chad. Her palms were sweaty, heart racing; she heard the pounding in her ears. She laid her head back against the headrest and closed her eyes, wiping her sweaty hands on her pants and pinching the bridge of her nose.

"Sasha," she was startled by the knock on the window. "Geez, you gave me a fright."

"Sorry, you ready to go?"

"Yes," she answered looking around and spotting Chad's car parked behind her.

"Okay, follow me," he said elated and briskly walked back to his car. Sasha followed Chad all through traffic and arrived at his apartment. He directed her to park in the guest parking next to his garage and waited by the side of the parking for her. She took a deep breath to steady her nerves, wiped her hands off on her pants' legs before changing out of her slippers into her stilettos, and only then got out of the car.

They walked side by side to the door. Sasha looked around at the complex, it was pretty. The yellow buildings neatly stacked four apartments per block. The gardens landscaped with peonies in an array of colours.

"You can come inside."

She laughed, "sorry, I was admiring the pretty flowers. This is such a beautiful complex."

Sasha walked inside and froze by the entrance as she took in the décor. The open-plan lounge and kitchen was tastefully decorated. An oversized brown leather couch placed against the one grey wall with a black and white portrait of an old car and a guitar on a wall mount, on the opposite wall hung a sixty inch television with two lamps lit demurely on each side. Her focus turned to the black rug on the floor, and followed the grain of the laminate flooring to the mahogany wood kitchen and breakfast nook. The granite tops sparkling in the glow of the down-lights.

Chad cleared his throat, "you okay?"

"Oh," she laughed, "I was just admiring your place. It is really beautiful."

"You sound surprised?"

"Well, you are a guy," she stuck out her tongue. "I thought there would be socks lying around."

"Yeah, I came home at lunch to clean."

"Seriously?"

"No, duh. I'm kidding."

"Ah well," she conceded and casually walked to the breakfast nook and took a seat.

"I hope you don't mind, I ordered some pizza," Chad said while he took two plates from the cupboard.

"I noticed when you got out of the car carrying that box. You scared I can't cook?" She laughed aloud. "Bang broek."

Shock flickered over Chad's face, "no, I... I..."

"It's fine Chad, don't stress about it."

He gave her a lopsided grin, "I didn't want you to be slaving in the kitchen on your first visit. This way we can just chill."

"But for the record, I can cook."

"I'm sure you can, but I would like you to visit again. I'll take advantage on another occasion." He winked and placed a plate on a placemat in front of Sasha and another next to her with two glasses and a bottle of coke. He walked around and took a seat next to Sasha, while she opened the pizza box and helped herself to a slice and offered one to Chad, who nodded and poured them each a drink.

"You really do have a beautiful place," Sasha complimented casting another glance around the room.

"Thank you."

"How long have you stayed here?"

"Three years."

"I've thought of moving from my parents' house but then I don't know," she shrugged. "Do you play?"

"Huh?"

Sasha gestured to the guitar mounted on the wall.

"Yes, I dabble.

"Would you play for me?"

"Sure, have you had enough?"

"Yes, thank you."

"You barely ate anything?"

"I had enough for now, thanks Chad." Sasha got up, took the plates and placed it in the sink.

"You don't have to do that?"

"You cooked, let me clean." Sasha laughed, "All done, see?"

They moved to the leather couch and sat on the opposite sides, a far berth between them.

"This couch is so comfy," Sasha said rubbing her hand over the leather.

"Yes, it is. I don't know how many times I've fallen asleep on it when I actually wanted to watch something."

"I can see that happening," Sasha agreed.

Chad slid closer to her, "this distance is just too much. Can we continue our conversation from this morning?"

"Yes, though there isn't much more. I had an epiphany and I see your point." She shrugged nonchalantly.

"That's big though. You'll finally see what I see."

She laughed, "Don't go crazy now. I am still me."

Chad laughed exposing the pink of his tongue, "that was quite an epiphany then, huh? And all brought on by jealousy?" He rubbed his chin pretending to think.

She play-slapped his hand.

"So on a serious note; you mentioned something about missing an opportunity?" They locked gazes.

She blushed profusely with a sharp intake of breath.

He slid even closer to her, "I like it when you blush," he said and touched her overheated cheek lightly with his right thumb, "does this mean, I can refer to you as my girlfriend then?"

Sasha swallowed hard staring at him wide eyed.

"I mean, I would love to be your boyfriend and like you said, we never made anything official. This is me, trying to rectify the situation?"

Sasha burst out laughing and nodded nervously.

"Situation, is that we have here?"

"Stop with the delay tactics, answer me," Chad reprimanded sternly.

"Yes," she answered breathlessly.

He pulled her closer and plunged his lips to hers and kissed her deeply, hungrily. Sasha was hesitant at first but after a few seconds her body instinctively responded to his. He pulled her onto his lap not breaking the kiss, hugging her tight to his body.

30

Two years later…

"I see the head!" Chad exclaimed horrified.

"Shut up," Sasha hissed between clenched jaws. Her legs firmly in stirrups sweat beads popping out across her forehead.

"Another firm push," the matron commanded in her ears, supporting her shoulders as she pushed.

"I don't think I can do this," she cried.

"You can do this baby," Chad whispered, his voice layered with unshed tears.

"One last push, it's almost over," the matron encouraged.

Chad held Sasha's face in both hands and steeled her with a look, "You can do this baby, you are the strongest woman I know," willing the words into her skull.

Sasha wiped the tears from her eyes with shaky fingers, "okay, I can do this," she said mustering all the will-power she could. She heaved and pushed with all the energy she had left, gritting her teeth. It felt like her body was being split apart. She shook her head, refusing to give up. Taking another deep breath and pushed with all her might.

Falling back to the bed, exhausted as the doctor proclaimed, "It's a girl."

The absence of pain was momentarily all Sasha could think of; again she started laughing and said, "That feels amazing." All the eyes turned to her questioning her sanity. But when they placed the baby covered in goo on her chest, tears started flowing anew. These tears were not born of pain or exhaustion; it was laced with unbridled joy.

Sasha looked from the big brown eyes of her daughter to Chad, who was hunched over the rail, his eyes red from the tears that spilled over his cheeks. Their gazes met and a bright smile spread over their faces as they both looked to the baby, suckling on her fingers.

"I love you, Sasha," Chad whispered hoarsely and placed a swift kiss on his new born baby's forehead cradled in her mother's arms.

"I love you too," She answered offering her index finger to the baby to hold.

"Marrying you was the best thing I've ever done in my life," he cried unashamedly, "you have made me the happiest man, and now a father." He brushed her hair back that was sticking to her face from the sweat and kissed her on her forehead, cheeks and lastly her lips. "You have taken my hand and led me into the light, you are my light. Thank you."

Sasha smiled exhausted turning her gaze to the other side of the bed where her mother stood, a tear rolling down her cheek, "I am so proud of you Sasha, luckiest baby to have a mother like you," she squeezed Sasha's hand and looked to Chad, "congratulations daddy."

Sasha watched the exchange between her mother and Chad as tears flowed over her cheeks once more. She had finally received her mother's approval and without even trying.

THE END

A mother and daughter relationship is one of the most important relationships there is. Children emulate what they see, so as mothers we must embrace our mistakes, nobody is perfect and remember that from the darkest places come the bravest souls. Rise above your past and move on gracefully. You are stronger and fiercer than you know. Teach your daughters how to be strong, how to love themselves and to not accept less than what they deserve. Loving yourself is not selfish, nor is it arrogant. Loving yourself is knowing your worth and once you know your worth, you will never accept a perfunctory love.

You are enough! Your worth is not determined by anyone. Your mistakes do not define you, how well you rise and move forward does. Embrace your darkness, BE UNAPOLOGETICALLY YOU!

You are beautiful!

About the Author

Nastasia Botha is a genre-hopping author who writes to inspire her readers through real, raw and sensual stories, inciting a kaleidoscope of emotions.

A true believer that even the dark side of love and life is worth embracing and exploring. Shining a light on those hidden desires no one dares speak of is the driving force behind her obsessive need to pen books of a somewhat unconventional nature.

Home for her is with her husband and two children in a small town "aan die gatkant van Gauteng" called Brakpan; where she enjoys swimming, singing, dancing and caring for her family.

An avid reader by nature, spending every second she has free; from being lost in the minds and thoughts of her characters; with her nose stuck between the pages of a book.

Acknowledgements

First and foremost, I want to say thank you to my Heavenly Father, for without Whom there is no me.

Deon, the love of my life, there are not enough words to describe how grateful I am to have you in my corner. Your unfailing love and unwavering support, is everything.

My babies, Gabriella and Justin, you are the world to me.

Dr. Nagdee, thank you for letting me talk your ears off and never tiring from answering all my questions.

Jarnine Roach, my eiese author bestie, thank you for your encouragement and always pushing me when I feel like quitting.

Jason King and Sheldon Botha, my friends and brothers, thank you for always supporting me, I appreciate you beyond measure.

Nerisa Manuel, our friendship has stood the test of time. We might not be related by blood but you are my sister in the truest sense, thank you for always having my back.

Last but by no means the least, everyone who has supported me through this journey, especially all my readers, Thank you, thank you, thank you.

Love always

NB

Photo credit: Cindy Segeel @ CNN Photography

Also by Author